Surprise Baby For The Secret Next Door Billionaire

A Small Town. Enemies To Lovers, Close-Pr  Romance

Aria McDow Publishing

Aria McDow

Surprise Baby For The Secret Next Door Billionaire

Cover: GetCovers

CONTENTS

1

C hapter One

SOFIA

Artsbridge is a small city in Maryland, located several hours away from Washington D.C. It's a beautiful, rustic place where the view consists of the Blue Ridge Mountains. It's where art and community converge in a way that make my soul come alive.

It's a Mecca for artists born and raised here, as well as for artists like me—transplants from other places.

Most of the time, the tourists far outnumber the folks who actually live here.

Although thousands flock to Artsbridge to partake in the mix of cultural, historical, and arts festivals, this is still a place where I can walk down the street and have people call me by my name.

My Uncle Carlos owns The Americana Del Sur Bakery—a medium-sized shop, nestled in the heart of Artsbridge.

The bakery is a cozy haven in the city and a cultural mixing pot. I like to think all of us who work here think the same and wouldn't have it any other way.

In Americana Del Sur, I have an amazing support network of co-workers and customers that help ease the pain of missing my family back home in Argentina.

How I love this place. Rustic charm mixed with modern eclectic is how I describe the feel of it. Exposed brick walls adorned with colorful local art, and worn, wooden floors that echo with history. There are tables for two, four and larger groups of more. There are board games, books, and local magazines within arm's reach of every table.

This is more than just a place to grab a morning bite—it's a welcoming, gathering place—a community hub.

It's 7 o'clock in the morning and time to open.

I make one last round of the bakery to see that everything is in place and check my watch again. Neither Eddie nor Ava have arrived yet for the start of the opening shift. I'm unconcerned. I know they'll be here, and I'll do my best to handle things until they arrive.

I inhale the aroma of freshly brewed coffee and baked goods and smile before I unlock the doors and turn the open sign around.

"Ready?" Gus, our resident baker, asks with a grin.

I grin back. "Yup. Let's do this."

I let up the blinds, turn the sign and unlock the doors. Customers are already waiting outside and I recognize many of them as regulars.

"Good morning, everyone!" I smile and wave them in.

"Wonderful to see you, Mrs. Greenly...C'mon in, Mr. Wallace...Yes, we have your favorite pastry, Renita..."

I head back behind the counter and begin manning the register and coffee machine solo. Gus, his broad frame hidden behind his flour-dusted apron, moves fluidly as he takes care of the pastries, sandwiches and breads in readiness for the breakfast rush.

I begin pumping orders through to the ticket machines at the coffee station and out to Gus. I stare back down the ever-increasing line of eager customers and swallow my panic. Where did all these people come from?

Gus must have read my internal panic by the expression on my face because he offers me an encouraging nod.

This is not the day I need two co-workers late at the same time, and yet that is exactly what I have. I struggle to keep up with making drinks and working the register, but I get on with it and keep smiling and being chatty.

That's when I notice *him*—a broad-shouldered, masculine, towering presence of impatience and irritation, almost at the end of the line. I know that scowl. What's he doing in here? I've lived next door to Lord of the Grump for six months without so much as a nod in my direction. Well, maybe not a nod but I have definitely caught him staring a few times.

I've tried to make conversation. No luck.

For the first time this morning I'm actually a little glad Eddie is late. If he sees the man he jokingly calls 'my grumpy husband' in here, I'll never hear the end of it. These thoughts race through my head as I automatically take orders, punch out tickets and turn to the coffee machine behind me to make the next lot of drink orders to go with the food Gus is handling.

I can't look at my neighbor. I have to focus on what I'm doing. He's just another customer. No big deal.

My treacherous eyes steal a glance and we make eye contact. *Shit! Why did I look at him?*

He's still scowling but the intensity in his eyes makes my stomach do a weird flip. My face heats up, and with no clue what else to do, I stupidly give him a huge grin.

I look back at the register and listen to the customer in front of me. This feels like forever and the line isn't getting any shorter. *Do not lose your shit now, Sofia.*

Smiling and nodding, I try to make each person feel like I'm interested in their conversation, and I am, I just don't have time for small talk with each of them.

I glance at the clock. Thirty minutes have passed. I look to Gus for reassurance and through the opening leading to the kitchen, I can see that Jordan, our junior baker, has arrived through the back entrance and is in the kitchen.

The bakery is pumping and I'm making hot drinks at a snail's pace. I'm super aware of my neighbor's presence in the long line and I glance at him again as I see him move sideways. He must be sick of waiting. Clearly a man with no patience.

I stare at him in shock as he suddenly strips off his linen blazer, revealing a sculpted physique of broad shoulders and bulging biceps in a body-fitting, short-sleeve button-up shirt. He hangs the jacket on the back of a chair, then he strides behind the counter to the coffee station as if he owned it.

He stares back at me for a split second. He's incredibly tall and broad this close up. His dirty blond colored hair is full, silky-looking, and at a length that makes me think he's not in a hurry to visit a barber. His eyes are a lighter brown than I'd noticed before. Somehow, he smells like spicy woodlands in the rain; maybe I'm dreaming.

He studies the long line of tickets I've put up and bangs out the drinks on the first docket with gruff efficiency that's surprising.

I look back at Gus and he raises an eyebrow but then shrugs and hand gestures as if to say, 'don't look a gift horse in the mouth'. In this case, a gift Barista.

"I'm on order thirty-one." Gus calls out to him.

My mystery neighbor swaps a few dockets around and gives Gus a double thumbs up as he gets to work. He doesn't utter a word to me as he places the drinks on the counter with the tickets, his briskness cutting through the morning chaos. Not a hint of friendliness towards me, just a determined focus to keep the line moving.

I keep taking orders while trying to ignore his aroma now mixed with fresh ground coffee. Ain't gonna lie, I've never smelt anything so good before, and finally, the line seems to have stopped actively growing. I hope he's gone before Eddie arrives.

As if Eddie Vasquez was waiting for that thought to enter my head first, he bursts through the door, a whirlwind of energy, color and drama; his apologies flying as fast as his feet.

"Sofia! So sorry I'm so terribly late—" He stops speaking when he spots who is making coffee. He stares hard back at me with his eyebrows almost touching the ceiling.

I frown and shake my head in an effort for him to just let it go.

He mouths slowly and deliberately, *what the actual fuck? Why is your grumpy husband making the coffee?* As he points towards my neighbor using his other hand as a useless cover-up.

"We're almost out of cups." The deep voice sounds from the coffee machine and I feel it resonate to my very core. I resist the urge to cross my legs as a strange, throbbing feeling shoots through deep, secret places. That's never happened before.

Eddie fans his face then pretends his hands are his penis exploding out of his cerise skinny jeans and I bite my lip hard to stop a burst of laughter escaping and encouraging Eddie.

Unfortunately, some people in my line of patrons see and giggle. The regulars love Eddie's over-the-top antics around here.

"I'll clear tables and stack the dishwasher," Eddie says and off he goes, his eyes locked on mine as far as he can strain his neck.

I try to focus on serving again. This is impossible, but somehow, I listen to my customers and continue pumping out tickets.

Moments later, Ava Montgomery, our glamorous barista and most recent addition to the team, sashays in. She's the only one who has never seen the man the others call my grumpy husband. She's heard plenty about him though.

She spots the mystery guy at the coffee machine and clearly panics. "Oh. My. God. Am I fired? I'm so sorry. I won't be late again." She wrings her hands. "Sofia, I need this job. Making coffee is the only thing I can do and I can't even do that very well. I'm just lucky you tolerate me." Her perfect smoky-look eyes are wide and shiny with tears.

"Um no...it's fine, Ava. You aren't— " I start to say, but then I'm interrupted.

"It's all yours." Mystery guy steps back around the counter. "Ticket fifty-six set up," he informs Ava as he picks his jacket up and places it over his arm.

"Okay. Thanks." Ava says as she flicks her blonde hair back and gives him a few blinks.

I think he almost smiled at her. He definitely stopped frowning. Whatever. Not like I care anyway.

Ava ties up her apron over her black designer pants and shirt. I envy her petite curves, blonde hair and blue eyes. She's a bombshell that turns every head when she walks in the door. It's not hard to see that she was a fashionista who easily rubbed shoulders with the rich and famous.

"I appreciate you." Her cute voice and giggle are also a complete contrast to my bossy tone and, at times, raucous laughter.

"No problem," he answers and, yes, that is a smile. Straight white teeth, his eyes crinkle at the sides. Then he gives her a wink. "Anytime."

"Ticket fifty-six has their food." I say quickly to jumpstart Ava into concentrating on the work needed. "Just waiting on their coffees, Ava." I don't care at all that he's giving her attention. Why would I?"

"Sure, Sofia. I'm on it." Ava smiles at me and I'm happy she's here learning a new skill. She's living proof that filthy rich men can cut you down as easily as they sweep you off your feet. The mud her ex and his high paid lawyers have dragged her through is criminal. Yet Ava remains focused on making enough here to feed her twin boys and keep a roof over their heads.

Meanwhile, Mr. Grump has abruptly reclaimed his spot at the customer side of the counter as if nothing has happened. He's standing there looking at me when I turn back to the register. I get a surge of everything I shouldn't through my entirety and my skin prickles with heat. I try and force my body to calm the fuck down.

"Double shot Latte, no sugar," he demands gruffly. "To go. I'm in a hurry and I've already wasted enough time."

Is he kidding me? Why didn't he just make his own while he was there? I punch in his order and type ASAP on the order so Ava knows to do that one first when it prints out. I suppose my dark hair and eyes, and tall, lanky shape don't interest him enough to smile at me, or even be polite. I want to be grumpy back and say that I didn't ask for his time. But he did step in and help and that was extraordinary.

I feel both gratitude for his help and annoyed at the mood he's casting toward me. But I remain gracious because I'm a glass-half-full kinda gal. "Thanks for the help. Much appreciated."

"Employ reliable staff if you can't handle the pace," he snaps.

I glare at him and he doesn't look away. My heartbeat is slamming as his golden-brown eyes remain fixed on mine. How dare he judge like that. Ava is struggling alone with twins and rent, and Eddie is his mom's caregiver and working to pay her medical bills. They can always be as late as they need to be. "I'm perfectly fine with the staff, and the pace."

He grunts a small noise of disbelief. "*Clearly...*" His sarcasm makes me want to flip him the bird, right up in his face. Again, no one has ever made me feel this way. Even in the depths of frustration my body reacts to him with unwanted tingling of my nipples and between my legs.

"Most people don't mind waiting a little," I counter calmly while wondering how long it is since he shaved and how he would look without his unruly facial hair. *Gah! Stop it, he's an ass. Who cares how he looks under all that scruff?* Ava places his drink and docket on the counter.

He pulls the take-out cup towards him. "I'm *not* most people."

"You are definitely right about that," I say, sliding a mini-sampler of my newest spiced dulce de leche creation his way. "On the house," I say with a smile, determined to keep the positivity high. Not everybody in the world has to like me. His loss.

He eyes the pastry like it's a snake that might bite him. "I never trust free offers. Usually con jobs."

I can't help but bristle at his attitude. "Suit yourself. There's plenty of people who appreciate what I have to offer." The moment the words leave my mouth, I regret the double entendre.

His slight raise of one eyebrow and sexy smirk sends a wave of heat to my cheeks and prickling down my neck.

Then he's back to frown-town and he pushes the pastry back my way. "I don't need your charity." He reaches into his pocket and pulls out a ten-dollar bill and hands it to me. "I just didn't want to wait till lunchtime to finally get my breakfast coffee."

I take the cash, push the pastry back across towards him, and place his change on the counter. "Just take the damn pastry." I finally concede the loss of my good mood. It's barely eight in the morning and this man has tipped me over the edge. "Give it away to Jerry on the park bench across the road if you're too *fragile* to try something new."

His frown deepens at my words and then he locks eyes with me as he picks up the single-bite pastry sample and stuffs it in his mouth in some sort of act of defiance. I give a close-lipped smile as smug satisfaction encompasses me; it seems he does have some buttons to push after all.

A split second later, his reactions are immediate and intense. He coughs, his face turns a shade of red I didn't think possible, and I panic as he clutches at his throat and in a hoarse cry he says, "Chili pepper!"

He doubles up, still coughing, and he grabs at the counter, wheezing and trying to clear his throat.

Holy shit! He's going into anaphylactic shock. I know it well. Seafood is the kiss of death for me. I spring into immediate action and fly around to the other side of the counter. I pull my EpiPen out of my bag. I never go anywhere without my allergy medication.

I jam the pen into his rock-hard thigh.

"Ow! What the fuck is that?!" He yells and collapses onto the ground. I kneel beside him, loosening his collar. Feeling for his pulse at his wrist, it's racing. He's still gripping at his thigh and gasping hard.

"Lie down." I push him back and pull his buttons open on his shirt so he can breathe easier. My hand may or may not have lingered too long in the dark chest hair, but I'll deny it in court. "It's okay. I'll call the ambulance," I reassure him. "I'm experienced with allergic reactions. I should've mentioned they have chili pepper in them."

I barely notice that people are gathering around, and the bakery has dropped into silence. Eddie is making high pitched noises from behind the counter.

"I don't have an allergy!" my reluctant neighbor barks as he stares around at the bakery patrons. "Go back to your breakfast. I'm fine."

I scramble away from him. Oh dear. I really called that one wrong.

"Oh, thank the Lord! I do not want any deaths on my watch," Eddie exclaims in a breathy voice as he hovers over us and then jumps to the register. "Nothing to see here folks. Who's next in line please?"

I'm feeling embarrassed and a little amused. So, shoot me. I always laugh at inappropriate times. "So, you're *not* allergic to chili?" I jump up and brush down my apron.

He stands up and steps to the side a little. "No." He rebuttons his shirt right up to the top as if he's just been violated and drags on his blazer like a protective shield. "Chili is just too damn hot. That's all."

Shit! "Oh wow. I'm so sorry. I just thought..."

"You just thought you could stab me with some poisonous dart." If his eyes were guns, I'd be peppered in bullets.

"It's an EpiPen." I stop myself from rolling my eyes. "Most people have no lasting effect from an accidental dose." I give him a small grin hoping to lighten his mood.

"I've already informed you that I'm *not* most people!" He growls low in a way that is somehow loud and also jolts a thrill deep into my center. "Geezus, I can't feel my leg." He rubs his thigh.

I resist the urge to rub his thigh for him and touch his arm lightly instead. "Look I'm really sorry. I've never seen such an animated reaction to chili before..." I say with a wide smile. Surely, he can see the funny side of this. No real harm done after all.

"Get away from me." He shrugs off my hand like it's the plague. "People like you should come with a warning," he grunts.

"*Like me*? You mean normal?" I really shouldn't bait him. "Let me make you a fresh coffee."

"Don't bother. I couldn't taste it after the Carolina Reaper pastry anyway," he grumbles as he turns to leave.

This is all just too much for me. I can't help myself but burst into peals of my too-loud laughter. I gasp for breath and my jaw is aching. He turns to glare at me as I regain some composure to speak. "What the hell? It's jalapeno. Barely even hot. My baby sisters eat them raw."

"I didn't come here to be attacked and ridiculed."

"If you *were* having an allergic reaction, I just saved your life. You're welcome."

"I was feeling fine until I came in here and experienced your incompetence."

"Maybe if you weren't so impatient in the first place none of this would have happened. You overreacted. Just admit it." I'm done with this pointless conversation and I'm not going to entertain his man-child attitude any longer.

"I should sue you."

"Go right ahead, one hundred percent of nothing is still nothing. But I'm happy to stand up in court and tell this story. Even Judge Judy needs a good laugh." I give him my biggest smile. "I owe you a coffee and a pastry, *of your choice*, next time you're in though."

"Next time! I barely survived this time. I won't be back." He gives me one last glare and hobbles out the door at the same time as my best friend, Bailey, walks in for her Friday shift.

I was also blessed to get Bailey as a cousin on my mother's side. She does a double take as my neighbor limps out the door and walks along the pavement. She looks back at me as the door swings closed. "Wait. What? Is that your grumpy husband?"

"Stop calling him that. I couldn't marry a man like that if my life depended on it."

2

C **hapter Two**

JULIAN

I pace the confines of my cluttered studio, a paintbrush in one hand, my phone in the other. The chaos of my latest abstract mocks me from the easel— nothing's coming together, not like it usually does. My mind's a tangled mess, all because of her—the fiery woman who's somehow embedded herself in my thoughts, into the very fiber of me, for the past six months.

I'm one, 'ah fuck it' away from calling my longtime manager and confidante, Miriam, and telling her to find out everything she can about the woman I now know as Sofia. Six months of telling myself I wanted to be alone and telling the world to go eff itself. By the world, I probably mean my family. Even though I love them all. I know what's best for me and I'm tired of everyone having an opinion about what will make me happy.

I arrived in Artsbridge, in the dead of night, six months ago, with the hope that no one would notice me. Life was kicking my ass and I badly needed a time out. I wanted a place where there was no pressure, no people, no unwanted memories or thoughts. I found that Artsbridge was where I could pour all that emotion and pain I was carrying into my dark abstract paintings.

In a tourist town, real estate is prime and places to live are expensive for ordinary folks. I found two, mountain view, side-by-side cottages and one was for rent at a very cheap price. I soon realized why.

I wasn't even sure the place was safe to live in, but my cottage definitely reflected my outlook on life at the time.

I was also assured that the other cottage was rented to some baker lady and I thought nothing of letting an old lady remain where she was. I ended up buying both cottages in a low-key, secret transaction.

Apart from making the heating and hot water safe and functional in them both, I'd left everything else unchanged.

Perfect, no one knew me here and Artsbridge wasn't really on the map unless it was the tourist season or had some interest in something artistic. The great exception to that was every two years when the Artsbridge Charity Arts Gala month happens.

Incredibly, artists from around the world descend upon Artsbridge to participate in this event, which is a mere two weeks away,

This was where my portrait work was discovered years ago and I've supported the model auction and exhibition activities ever since. My family supports many charities and, as the highest profile law firm in D.C., being active in national and international charity events is something we've always done.

I'd successfully faded into the background here until the day I saw that the elderly baker woman I imagined as my next-door neighbor, wasn't elderly at all, but rather the most exquisite-looking woman I had ever seen.

She was also the next-door neighbor with the nerve to start drawing me out to the forefront by constantly intruding on my solitude with her hellos, waves, and smiles. Does she not get that I'm not interested in getting close to anyone, especially a woman as drop-dead gorgeous as her? I've been burned too many times by women with that type of look.

She's no baker, so what is she even doing in that bakery? She could be on runways across the world. She beats any A-Lister that I've ever met and I've known most in the past ten years.

Sofia. The name suits her long dark hair and flashing dark eyes. She's tall and lean but somehow her curves hit in all the right places.

I'd followed her one time, to see where she went in the early hours of the morning. Maybe I'm slightly unhinged, I could have just asked her. But I don't want to seem interested, and I don't want the press to find out where I am, so laying low is imperative.

Then, this morning, I went right in and lined up. I don't even know why but I couldn't stop myself. I'm not worried about being recognized because I barely even recognize myself in the mirror these days. Maybe I was even going to say hi and chat about the weather.

My cock firms a little as she floods my thoughts. *No, I'm not thinking like that.*

But she was under the pump, and making coffee is something I've often done at many events. Imagine having *the* Julian Blackwood, playboy son of billionaire Blackwood attorney powerhouse in Washington D.C., making your morning coffee.

People, mostly women, came in droves and before I fell in love and married, I'd lapped up every second living up to my playboy image. Before I married, that was an image I needed to forget and a life I wanted to leave behind. But the wife I loved cheated on me, and met her death in a speedboat accident along with her lover.

Those revelations were bad enough but the news the autopsy showed rocked me to my core.

There had been a tiny baby, growing undetected. DNA testing revealed that it was my baby. Something I'd never even thought I'd wanted, and now the pain of losing all of that possibility was just too much. Why couldn't it have been her lover's baby? I push the thoughts aside. I'm not that person, am I? I have no clue right now and this effort to find myself has only made me feel more lost.

My mind and body feel shrouded in dark clouds until Sofia comes into view. When she does, every part of me wakes up and takes notice.

I acted like an idiot. Just should have said hello and offered to help. It didn't have to be a big deal. No, it didn't have to, but it was. I wanted to just pull her into my arms and kiss her. I wanted to tell her how the smell of her keeps me awake at night and how everything about her infiltrates my day. Now I just want to paint her, and I know I will go back into that bakery and see her again.

I can't suppress a smile as I rub my thigh and recall her laughter at my presumed medical emergency. Once upon a time I'd have laughed over it as well. I haven't been that person for a very long time. But god, she has everything I find physically attractive in a woman. I can't stop remembering her long, lithe body close to mine. I imagined my hands squeezing all of her generous curves and I can't get the thoughts out of my head. My cock reacts again and I push the thoughts away. Relationships are not for me and there's no way one time with her would ever be enough.

I video call Miriam; my agent, former lead investigator on my cases, former security, and longest friend. We have a lot of history. I could never shake her off and now I wouldn't dream of wanting to. I wait for Miriam to pick up, rehearsing what I'll say so I don't sound like an obsessed stalker. She's due here tomorrow to pick up my latest finished work and I'm hoping she can help me out.

"Julian, to what do I owe the pleasure? Another secret abstract of anger ready for the world, I know, but tell me you're going back to portrait painting... Make my day, please," the diminutive form of Miriam appears, looking over the top of her black-framed glasses.

"Not quite," I start, pausing to choose my words carefully. "There's someone I need you to find out about—a woman from the bakery near my studio. Americana Del Sur. She's... intriguing."

Miriam chuckles, the sound rich and knowing. "Ah, I knew your penis would get sick of hiding away eventually. Intriguing, huh? That's a first from you in a long while."

"It's not like that. My penis is just fine." Miriam has no filter and you always know where you stand with her. "But she's got this presence, something about her and—" I stop, suddenly aware of how passionate I sound. I don't want her thinking this is anything but an artistic eye wanting to paint a subject. "I haven't wanted to paint a portrait in a very long time, and just maybe— "

"Say no more. I'm on it," Miriam interjects, the promise of me re-entering the art world and becoming semi-normal again hanging in the air. "Are we talking a full background sweep?"

I swallow, I want to say no but I can't. "Yes. Be discreet."

"What's her name?"

"Sofia. That's all I have but she's the tenant who lives next door, so the details will be in the rental documents. I'm not sure why she lives in such a dump."

"Probably all she can afford."

I contemplate that for a moment. "I may need to do some improve-ments to these cottages."

Miriam chuckles knowingly again. "Let me guess, bedrooms first?"

"It's not like that. I've changed. You know that."

"You didn't need to change. You just needed to admit who you are and live life on your own terms."

"Who I am is not an option. I'll never be part of the law firm juggernaut my father wants his first-born heir to be."

"I'm talking about the artist. The portrait artist. The man who needs love like any other man on this earth but is just too stubborn to admit it."

"My portraits were popular because of my last name."

"That's not true. You know how the media is. You cannot put any credence on what's said."

"They are right. At least the abstracts sell, and no one knows who really paints them, so that proves my work is worth something."

"It proves you are driven by your ego. You can't live in denial forever. Eventually it will come back and bite you in the ass."

"Same shit, different day. Are you going to do this for me or not?"

She sighs. "Okay. Sofia. Works at bakery. Lives next door. Any other details?"

"Isn't that enough or have you lost your touch?

"I can still take you out before you've even realized I'm in the building."

I know it's true. Miriam may look like a fifty-something lady from a tearoom, but she can use every object on the tea cart as a lethal weapon, and if they all fail, she still has her bare hands. Besides I think she's older than fifty-something. I'd met her in a martial arts class when I was barely eighteen, we got along, and I offered her a job.

There was a hell of a lot about Miriam that I didn't know then. I'd place bets on there still being just as much that I don't know now. Then and now, but her attitude towards me was refreshing. She didn't treat me like anything special because of my name. She was just as happy to put me on the ground in training—with a foot across my throat—as she was any Tom, Dick, or Harry. I liked that.

Funny thing is, I don't officially use security anymore but she's still here. Now she's my agent for the abstracts. I'm not questioning it too hard, I'm not sure what my life looks like without the surety of Miriam Graythorne in it, and I don't want to find out anytime soon.

I laugh. "I don't doubt that. Just see what you can find out. I don't want to cause her any trouble. From her accent, I'm sure she is here from another country but she speaks English fluently. I'm just curious and I would love to paint her."

"Anything that gets you out from under the cloud of doom is okay by me. You know, it's okay to make a friend."

"A friend?" I really haven't thought about that. Friends aren't something I've bothered with. I never had anything in common with anyone enough to want them around that much. At college I was a fish out of water. I wasn't interested in talking sports or studying high-powered attorney cases. I just worked on my art in my spare time.

"Yeah, you know, someone you enjoy being around. It doesn't always have to be black and white. Friends can fit into the gray," Miriam explains.

"I'm not sure that's a good idea. Wouldn't I need to be honest about who I am?"

"Eventually, perhaps. But you can have friends who know nothing about you. It's about enjoying the moment. You aren't seriously thinking you can keep up this pretense for much longer? Someone will spot you eventually. I'm surprised you've lasted this long."

"I'm doing fine and I've lasted this long without friends. Why start now?" I sometimes wonder what it would be like to have the camaraderie I can see in the bakery. I have that with my four younger brothers who constantly bust my chops, but no, I don't need friends.

"There are people who would give anything to have a life again and here you are wasting yours. I think it's time you used what you have to help others instead of brooding over things you can't change. Charity work always made you smile so why don't you fake it till you make it?"

"Fake it till you make it? Are those your final words of wisdom?"

"Works for me every time."

For the first time, it occurs to me that Miriam will have had pain or loss in her life. I mean, she's such a constant, but I've never asked her about her personal life. "Miriam, I've never told you and I should have. You know you can come to me if you need anything, ever."

"See? You can have friends and not know anything about them. It's okay to do that."

I feel she's just trapped me into something. "Look, I'll go see her again. What can it hurt? We have similar interests and there's a lot about the art world I can show her."

"And apologize for whatever it is you did."

"I didn't do anything but help." Damn her, she knows me too well.

Miriam's dry chuckle shows she doesn't believe me. "Help? *Sure.* Look, if she doesn't know who you really are, then she must just want to be your friend because she likes your personality. Ego appeased."

"This is not about you being right and me being wrong..." A long-fought rivalry that she is way ahead on. I stare at her, "Is it?"

"Of course not because, we both know, I'm always right."

I shake my head and smile. Miriam is the closest person I have to a friend, of that I am certain. Let me know as soon as you find out anything. I hope Sofia is who she says she is."

"None of the women you've ever been with were right for you. Maybe it's time you looked under a few different rocks. We aren't meant to walk this earth alone," Miriam says, she is better at reading between the lines than anyone else I've ever known.

"I'm never falling in love again. I don't care what you say. Walking this earth alone is what I want."

3

C hapter Three

SOFIA

The line at the bakery is out the door again the next morning but we have all hands on deck and I've been in early and gotten everything prepped. Lucky really, because my head's spinning with a bunch of stuff about my family back home and my future here as I talk with Uncle Carlos in the back office.

I'm desperately trying to wrap my mind around what my father's older brother is telling me.

"Tio, are you saying the bank will foreclose if you don't have that payment at the end of the month?" I stare at Uncle Carlos in disbelief as he paces back and forth.

His clothes are expensive and well-made but several years old. Today, they look almost rumpled and I know he'd rather be dead than caught not looking sharp. At my height, I almost tower over him. He's so like my father in appearance, and so unlike him in temperament.

He nods his head with it hair-color and thickness now faded from its former glory. "I'm sorry, Sofia. I thought my numbers would come up."

"Can't you borrow some off your rich friends?"

"Then they will know I'm not like they are," he says stubbornly.

"You aren't like they are. Your bank account can't keep up with millionaires. Just ask one of them for a loan. I'm sure fifty thousand dollars is small fry to them."

Uncle Carlos continues his pacing. "I can't. I've already borrowed one hundred thousand because I knew my numbers were coming up on the next spin."

"What? My mind is reeling. "You borrowed the money to save the bakery plus some and then you lost that money too? So now we need one hundred and fifty thousand? Oh, *Tio* Carlos. We need a miracle."

"You can get married. I've introduced you to many men who would marry you. Your father asks me constantly, why won't Sofia help and marry one of your friends?" His dark eyes almost plead with me.

Frustration builds inside me but, despite everything, he is my uncle and I speak respectfully "Because Sofia isn't a commodity you marry off for money and status. No female is."

"It could be so much easier for you, Sofia. You don't have to be working your ass off every day. You could marry the kind of money that means you or your family never have to worry about money, education, or living your dreams again."

I know he's coming from a place of love, but these are the stereotypes I need to break for the sake of my sisters and all the youth born into this way of thinking. Change will come through the children who will lead later in life and I want to do what I can to help children in my home country break free of old-fashioned stereotypical roles.

"I want to make my own way, *Tio*. You must understand. You came here with *Tia* Rosa and you both worked this business into a success. *Tia* worked as hard as you. I will never marry any rich man to be a trophy on his arm. I want love. Real love. Like you and *Tia*."

Tio Carlos hangs his head. He looks down and I know he feels genuinely sorry about the situation he has us in again. It's like he's stuck on a hamster wheel, and he can't break away.

"This bakery would be nothing without your Tia Rosa. I am nothing without her. I've failed her. I've failed everyone."

I put my arm around his shoulders.

Aunt Rosa passed away three years ago. That was part of the reason I knew it was time to ask Uncle Carlos to sponsor me. He needed someone to fill the huge gap she left. I may have done that in the bakery, but I hadn't in his personal life. Being someone he isn't took him over. Trying to be good enough. Everything I'd tried to get him to understand that he was a ticking timebomb had failed. Now the bomb had gone off and somehow, we need to clean up the mess.

"That's not true. You got lost. That's all. Look at how you've made my life better. I have many friends. I get to bake all the time and I love everyone who works here. If I can get that money, somehow, *Tio*...will you keep Americana Del Sur open?"

"I don't know, Sofia. I'm tired. I need to get away for a while. Money from a sale will help me do that. It's time I went back home and grieved properly. The easy way is to let the bakery go to clear the debt. Maybe, deep down inside, that's what I wanted all along. I just couldn't admit it."

I feel for him in this moment. Apart from me, he has no family here. Aunt Rosa couldn't have children. Uncle Carlos was the first in our family to believe in his dream and he'd helped so many in our family try a different life. "*Tio*, please. Don't rush into anything. Give me a chance to crunch the numbers; maybe you can get a business loan or something."

Tio Carlos is silent for moment. Then, as if he has decided something, he speaks. "If you can come up with the money to clear the debt;

you can run the bakery and control the bank account. I'll be a silent partner."

I don't know why, but I breathe a sigh of relief. It's not as though I'm expecting my Tio's offer to actually happen, or even if that's what I want. My long-term goals are about making a living from art. But if it gives him hope and maybe this could work, everyone here will still have a job. I have to try. "Let's not rush into any decisions, Tio."

"I've had a long time to think about this, Sofia. I will sell the bakery unless you can take it over because I'm tired."

The conversation has reached a temporary stalemate and there's nothing more to say, except, "I understand, Tio Carlos." I give him a hug.

It's been a real grind, keeping this ship afloat while Tio Carlos is out there playing high-roller with money he doesn't have. But everything else about being here has been a godsend in my life. I have so many friends. My work family is amazing. Every single person here needs their job. Shutting down? Not on my watch. This place means the world to them, and heck, it's my rock too, right now.

Honestly, when I think about it, I've got it pretty good. I'll tell Gus and all the staff after we close today. Maybe we can find a solution together. I head back out to clear tables and see where I'm needed.

My mind is churning. I get to work cleaning up tables, wiping down the register, and wiping down the counter. "Take a break, Eddie. Then come back to man the coffee machine while Ava has her break."

"Sure." He is still looking at me. "Are you okay?"

"We'll all talk after shift." I give him a smile. "I'm fine. Let's get ready for the lunch rush."

"No problem." He goes off to con his daily favorite sandwich from Gus.

"Actually, Ava, you may as well take a break now. It's pretty quiet."

"Thanks, Sofia. I need to call my babysitter. She's new and the twins were being a little rebellious this morning before I left. I hope she got them to kindergarten okay."

"No problem. Let me know how it all went," I say as she goes off out back. I clean down the coffee station and machine.

"Hello." The word and timbre resonate deep within my core.

I stop cleaning and turn around. Light brown eyes take my next breath away as his smile almost makes my heart stop. Eddie goes dancing past behind him, sandwich in one hand and thumbs up to me. "Oh, hey," he says as he stops and leans in nearer to my neighbor. "How's the leg?"

"Great, thanks." He looks at Eddie as he answers and then his gaze is back on me. Eddie raises his eyebrows and fans his face.

I glare at Eddie and he takes the hint and leaves. "Hi," I say, trying to sound like all is well and I'm just serving another one of my regulars. "Double shot Latte to go?"

"Actually," he asks, "can you join me for a second. Do you have time?"

Eddie is back again. "*Sure* she can. I'll bring over some drinks."

I glare at him for even being close enough to hear. He just waggles his eyebrows at me from behind my neighbor. "Okay. Fine. Yes, let's go sit. I'm due for a break anyway." What can he possibly want to say to me? I step out from behind the counter and sit at the closest empty table.

"I'm Jack," he holds out his hand before he sits.

I take it in mine and I swear the imprint of his fingers will be burned into my skin forever. "Sofia. Nice to officially meet you, neighbor."

"I think I owe you an apology."

"For overreacting yesterday? No problem," I say with a smile.

"No. For never saying hello and introducing myself when you've been friendly."

"Oh. Okay. That's fine. I get that some people like their personal space." Eddie drops two lattes off on the table and leaves again. I bet he's still within earshot. I take a sip of the beverage. The coffee tastes perfect and I didn't realize how much I needed the break until now.

He laughs. "You do? I'd never have guessed."

"If you are referring to yesterday, I really thought I was helping. I suffer from allergies that are life-threatening and I never take chances."

He puts both his hands up, "I get it. But you could have asked first instead of jumping to conclusions." He takes a mouthful of coffee. "This coffee is great."

If he was trying to change the subject, he failed. I spoke again. "You could also have not over-reacted to the jalapeno. What was I supposed to think?" I don't know why I can't be gracious about this. My pulse is racing and I know I'm as red as fire. No one has ever affected me this way.

"Look, thanks for the coffee." He abruptly stands up, frowning, and pulls a five-dollar bill from his pocket. "This was a mistake."

Then he leaves and I'm just sitting here with my eyes wide. He really has a short fuse.

Unbelievable. Pity he isn't a little less volatile. Well, who am I to talk? This man has me so confused. I have all sorts of feelings pumping everywhere at the moment. Mom always told me I'd know when I met the man I want to give my V card to. And if pure sexual attraction is it, I just had him sitting across from me.

I'd also made a pact not to settle for anything less and that had extended my virginity way longer than I'd intended. Of course, this pact is also the hot topic among my co-worker friends, except Gus who is way too old-school and respectful to comment on that subject.

I swallow the rest of my coffee just as Bailey swoops in to sit down. She only works Friday morning, so she's just come in for a gossip session, no doubt.

"Um.... did I just miss something epic?"

"Yesterday, I thought he was in anaphylactic shock and I used an EpiPen on him. He flipped out. I swear, Bailey, my heart was beating like I just ran a marathon. I thought he was gonna die and all he could do is say I overreacted when he was the one who overreacted." I let out a huff, still trying to process my inner turmoil. "It's not like jalapenos are that hot, sheesh."

Bailey leans in, her curiosity piqued. "Okay. But why was he here just now and why were you sitting with him over coffee?"

I shrug. "He asked if we could have a chat. Wanted to say sorry or some shit. But he left in a huff again." I know my face is on fire but I'm hoping Bailey doesn't think anything of it. "I've never met a man who makes me feel so... so... aggravated." I struggle to find a word that doesn't describe what I'm actually feeling.

"*Aggravated?* Is that what they're calling it now?" Bailey grins at me. Then her eyes open wide. "Oh. My. God! He's the pact-breaker, isn't he?"

Eddie drags over another chair and sits, crossing his long, slim legs like a super model. "He is so, so, *so* the pact-breaker. I thought it was just me, but you see it too, don't you Bailey? And, I am here for *all* of it."

She nods at him and they both grin at each other. "Me too. *All* of it!"

"I'm still here, you know." I wave my hands at them. "No need to discuss me like I'm not."

Jordan, fresh from baking cinnamon rolls, arrives and pulls over a seat, turns it backwards and sits astride it, her heavily-tattooed arms resting across the back. "Do you lot ever do any work?" She teases.

"It's break time. And grumpy husband has just been back. Did you see him?" Eddie asks Jordan.

"I was elbows deep in dough, so no. Spill the tea. Did he have his leg amputated?"

Yesterday has clearly been discussed.

"His name is Jack," I tell them.

"*Jack* is the pact-breaker." Eddie grins.

"No way!" Jordan high-fives Eddie and Bailey at the same time.

"Way!" Eddie and Bailey answer in unison.

"We can't be sure this isn't an alternate universe," Jordan says with a frown. "Maybe I'm asleep and dreaming."

"I really have no hope with you all." I'm trying not to smile. "This subject, and break, is over. Let's get back to work."

Eddie and Ava go and set up the tables for lunch and restock as needed.

"I really just came in to see if anyone wants to go to the club tonight," Bailey says.

"No club for me," Jordan says. "I'm done for the day. Gus has left already. Day off tomorrow. I love Sundays without hangovers." Jordan smiles and runs a hand through her short-cropped hair. "See you Monday." She stands up and gives me and Bailey a fist-bump. "You know, Sof, if you're feelin' it with your grumpy husband...I mean, Jack, go with it. But, no pressure. Always your choice. Not anyone else's."

"Thanks, Jordan. I appreciate the support but it's not like that—at least I'm pretty sure it isn't—and he has such a short fuse I don't think he could ever be in the same room as me for long."

She grins. "He's probably just so into you, he doesn't know how to handle it. Not that I'm into men, but honey, that man is disgustingly hot!" She puts back the chair at the next table and leaves.

"He's molten lava," Eddie agrees as he conveniently swings past. "I'd do him in a second." Then he's gone.

It's just Bailey and me again. "Honestly, I don't think I've ever come across anyone so... well, moody, I guess is the word." I can't help the smile that spreads across my face. "He *is* kinda hot though." I fan my face with my hand.

Bailey smirks, pointing at me. "Kinda hot? That is the understatement of the year. Even with all that crazy hair."

"Mmmm, I was wondering what he'd look like clean shaven." I say quietly without thinking.

"Sounds like someone's got a crush on their grumpy husband," Bailey teases.

"Crush? No way. It's like... like a lightning bolt, you know? Just zaps me out of nowhere. But I definitely don't have a crush." I shake my head. "Can you please just call him Jack?"

"Of course. Jack." She smiles at me. "Sofia, I think getting zapped by a grump is the universe's way of telling you it's time to lose that V card and go be the best version of yourself. Maybe you're getting desperate." She laughs. "But seriously, anyone who can make you hot and bothered like this is worth at least another look."

I can't quite suppress a grin. "Yeah, he kinda rocked my world for a minute there. But I have bigger things to worry about. This bakery is on the verge of bankruptcy and I need to find one hundred and fifty grand pronto."

"Wow. That's a lot. Let me guess, *Tío* Carlos?" Bailey shakes her head.

"I think he's ready for a change. He wants to sell but if I can come up with the money, he'll let me run this business. I'm not sure, though. It's not what I saw for myself, but if this place closes, none of us has a job. And where will everyone go to get their social fix?"

"You can't fix everything, Sof."

"I can try. I mean, I just want to explore all options before it actually has to shut down."

Bailey looks thoughtful before a gleam appears in her eyes. "Well..., the grand charity auction is in two weeks. There's still time to enter the nude art model auction part like I've been telling you for months. This could be your big break. It could also net you some serious money for the business that you represent."

"Not as much as I need, surely?"

"I've heard that some private agreements easily run into that amount and more."

"For little old Artsbridgers? Unlikely."

"What are you talking about?" Bailey says. "It launched that reclusive billionaire guy's art career. What's his name? Julian Blackwood?"

"Yeah, I think so. He's the same one who always went to such extremes to keep from being photographed. The only things I know about him for sure is that he was a billionaire before he was a famous artist, his family are old money, and that his portraits are outstanding." Blackwood's talent was one of the reasons I decided to focus on portrait work. I wanted to capture a subject's essence the way he does. He's an expert at that. I frown, "But he hasn't painted anything new for ages."

"I read somewhere that he's disappeared actually. No one knows where he is since the scandal broke about his wife dying in that speed boat accident with her lover."

"I don't blame him. Imagine having your personal family drama being scrutinized and dissected for entertainment. It would be awful. Anyway, back on topic: you're right. I *have* heard that some bids make the thousands, though many have confidentiality clauses so we'll never really know."

I shake my head. Who am I kidding? "This event is huge and artists around country—and even the world—descend every two years upon this little city for this art auction. They participate right alongside popular locals who have a story to tell or a lot of life experience. In comparison, I'd be an unknown in a sea of knows. I doubt I'd make any money. I'm truly inspired by some of the amount of unique talent in this small city, but to presume I'm part of that fabric yet is a little much.

"You're a local; you've been here almost two years. Everyone loves you and the bright spark you bring to their day. To this place. To all of our lives. Don't sell yourself short. Yes, it's a big deal, but this is still a local event so you have every right to enter."

"I don't know, Bailey. It seems like a desperate, not to mention presumptuous, measure."

"This could be your big break. If nothing else, you get some money, the bakery gets some money, and once the artwork is sold, a charity of your choice gets money. This might be the platform you need to start up support for kids' education in Argentina."

"The thing is, I want to be the artist, not the model."

"What better way to get into the circle? No one has ever been chosen for the nude model section. Rumor has it, that it's screened by famous artists and photographers, some have ticked the box but no artist has taken up the option. I bet they'd snap you up."

I hesitate, the idea of modeling nude stirs a mix of excitement and apprehension inside me. "I dunno, Bailey. The whole nude thing... my

Uncle Carlos may be desperate but he's very old-fashioned. I can only imagine some strict morals taking an inconvenient time to surface. Besides, you know, what if my future kid sees it? My sisters..."

Bailey grabs my hand, squeezing it reassuringly. "Hey, you'll cross that bridge if it comes. Come on, where's our Sofia? The one who is always positive? It can't hurt to try, right? I think you can change your mind about the nude part anyway."

"Okay, okay. I'll do it. For the bakery, for my art, and maybe... to prove to myself I can." A rush of excitement floods me. Why shouldn't I? There's no reason why this couldn't be my big break. If it isn't, I haven't lost anything by trying.

"Hooray! Then, you make some A-list connections, and make some real money. You could buy this place. Bring your mom to run it and focus on your art world domination. Get a permanent residency. I mean, modeling is an artform in itself. You have what it takes. You just need to apply your positive, stubborn attitude to it and you can always focus on your art later." She shrugs like it's the simplest thing in the world and she can't believe I haven't already thought of all this.

She's right. I need to apply my positive attitude to what I want. The only thing stopping me is me. "It does sound simple when you put it like that. I've never been ashamed of my body, so why start now?"

Bailey's grin could light up the room. "That's my girl."

"Okay, I need to get ready for the lunch rush. I'll fill out and send in the application online tonight after I close up. I promise."

4

C hapter Four

JULIAN

I stand outside the bakery, feeling like a complete idiot. Here I am, Julian freaking Blackwood, nervous as shit about knocking on a bakery door after hours. Why didn't I just say I was sorry to overreact earlier today when I came in? Now, I cannot get her off my mind. I can't even paint the stupid abstracts. My brush strokes always come back to outline Sofia.

The "CLOSED" sign stares back at me, but there she is, moving around inside. Before I can talk myself out of it, I tap on the glass, half-hoping she won't hear. But she does. She walks over, surprise etched across her face, then shifts to something softer, something inviting, as she unlocks the door.

"We are closed," she says. "But I have a little finishing off to do. Come in."

"Sorry, I just … needed caffeine," I blurt out, stepping inside. Damn, I sound foolish. "I can go if it's too much of a bother."

Sofia locks the door again and pulls down the door blind. "No drama. I was about to make my nightcap coffee. I should be gone by now anyway. Sorry if I upset you earlier. I did overreact with the EpiPen yesterday."

"Apology accepted. I overreacted as well. Yesterday and today." For a moment, I quietly watch her work as she froths the milk and I speak before the silence grows awkward. "Truth is, I've been less than civil to you since I moved here. Mostly it's just the funk I'm in. It isn't you."

"I know it's not me." She smiles a wide smile and her dark eyes twinkle in a way I find utterly enchanting. Then she winks. "I'm teasing. Apology accepted."

I take the coffee she hands me. "I'll drink to that."

She raises an eyebrow. "Is that so? Can I interest you in a slug of this?" Sofia holds up a bottle of butterscotch schnapps. "My regular nightcap for Saturday shifts."

"Sure. But if I cough, I'm not allergic to it, okay?" I say, as she pours the schnapps to top up my coffee.

There she goes with that laugh again. I fight the desire to lose my hand in her hair and turn that laugh into a gasp with a kiss. But I'm making a friend, and friends don't do that. She sits at a small table and I follow suit. "What's your story, Jack?"

Jack is what my family called me as a boy, so I'm not exactly lying about my name. But my father put a stop to it once I went to college to become the great Julian Blackwood. "I keep to myself. I like it that way."

"Yet, *here* you are. Why?"

I shrug. "Great question. I guess I miss chatting with someone fun."

She nods but I can tell she's still suspicious of my answer. "Just a man who jumps behind counters and gets into chili pepper incidents, huh? What do you do in all this spare time being a loner?" Her dark gaze is curious, playful yet probing.

Her directness is quite refreshing, but my mind races for any answer that doesn't scream *billionaire with issues*. "I'm an artist."

"Oh, cool. You're in the right place for that. Have you had any showings?"

"Not really. But I do sell my abstracts."

"How awesome."

"And you? Always wanted to run a bakery?" I ask, to move the subject off me.

"No, the baking is a bonus. Something my mother taught me. Makes me feel closer to her." Her attention drifts off for a second. "This place...it's more of a family obligation than a passion. But family is everything to me and I love it here. One day, I'd like to make a living from my art."

"So, you're an artist as well? A fellow artist? And a most beautiful one at that. Something in my soul lights up a bit. "What medium?"

"Oils, canvas. Portraits, mostly. But I wouldn't call myself an artist just yet. Maybe someone who dabbles."

Portraits. Same as me. Quite the coincidence. But I can't say anything because if she's into art and particularly portraits she will have heard of and seen Julian Blackwood paintings, I'd think. "It's a tough game. Where are you from?"

"I was born in Buenos Aires, Argentina. My family lives there. Uncle Carlos, my father's brother and his wife, fled Argentina decades ago to escape some pretty bad times. He owns this place and I've been here almost two years."

"I see. You'll get permanent residency?"

She nods. Her look is distant for a few seconds. "Hope to. There's a lot I'd like to achieve here and for my siblings back home. I'd like to help support education and more choices for the next generations."

"You're very ambitious. I like that. Determined people succeed."

She smiles. "If determination were all it took, I'd have zero problems. I seem to have hit a block. Nothing I paint feels right. I haven't picked a brush up in weeks. How did you break out and sell your art?"

I consider how to answer this. "I knew someone in the industry who liked my stuff. They give me financial backing, and exhibit and sell my art for me."

"So, it's not *what* you know it's *who* you know..." her brow creases as she speaks.

"Partially. There has to be some merit to your work as well. But the market can be...well, just weird. You just never know what the world will deem to be the next big thing."

"Sounds like a lot of luck as well then."

"Yes, and timing. It's very hard to quantify any creative career. Perhaps I could take a look at some of your work sometime..."

She looks at me, her eyes burning into mine. "You would? I mean, really?"

"I'm no expert but if you can take some constructive criticism, it might help." I would genuinely like to help out if I can.

"I'd be grateful to have another artist take a look. Friends and family are always going to say they love it. I just want to know that it's okay from someone who isn't personally invested in me in some way." She shrugs. "It sounds selfish and petty."

"No. I get it. I know exactly what you mean. I'd love to take a look but no guarantees." I'm lost in her eyes again. "There's a lot of great art exhibitions in the area. We should go and see some of them. If you get time."

"You'd want to do that?"

"Sure. I can take a day off from being a loner. It would be kinda cool to hang with someone who gets art for a change. You can learn a lot from other artwork and its history. Maybe it's what you need to get the creativity flowing again."

"Thanks. I really needed a boost today." Her hand finds mine and the warmth of the touch spreads over me like sunshine on a frosty field.

I'm so drawn to her. Despite myself I lean in a little closer and she does the same. Her eyes are wide and encased in the longest, curved natural lashes I've ever seen. The vanilla floral scent washes over me and I want to taste her kiss more than anything I've ever wanted. It's dangerous ground. I'm meant to be making a friend. I'm supposed to be keeping myself to myself.

My heart pounds in my ears as we draw ever closer and she closes her eyes.

Then something bangs out back, making a jarring noise, and her eyes snap open again and she jumps up off the chair. "Who's there?" she calls out.

"Sofia? Why are you still here?" A short man with silver hair and the last vestiges of dark color at the sides, appears from the kitchen.

"*Tio* Carlos. You scared the hell out of me." Sofia clutches her chest. "I'm about to leave. I had a late customer and we had coffee together. This is Jack."

The small man eyes me up and down. "I see. I hope there's nothing else going on here, Sofia. You know how your father feels about you being with men alone."

"I choose my own friends, *Tio*. But thank you for caring." She smiles at him and he nods and resumes glaring at me.

"I'm just leaving," I say and head for the front door. "Thanks for the late coffee, Sofia. Nice to meet you, Carlos."

"You're welcome. I'll let you out," Sofia says as she walks towards me. Carlos doesn't answer.

When we are alone at the door I whisper, "I'll wait for you."

"No, I'm fine," she whispers back.

"I'll walk you home. I know it's not far and you've done it a million times, but I'd like to. We can sort out where we should go visit."

"Okay. I'll grab my bag. Thanks."

I wait outside on the pavement and in about five minutes, she's beside me. "I came out of the back door."

Spinning around, I smile, "you shouldn't sneak up on someone like that."

"Sorry, but it's okay. I'm here to protect you on the way home now."

I laugh and that feels good.

"Jack, in there, I know we had a moment. But I'm not looking for anything serious. I'm happy to be friends. I have a lot going on in my life and I'm not looking to complicate things."

I appreciate her directness. So refreshing. I don't think anyone would ever not know where they stand with Sofia. I feel as if the dynamic has already shifted between us. I crook my arm towards her. "No problem. Come on, we can have a quick look at your work."

She hooks her arm through mine. "I won't say no to that. I have some wine."

"I have some steak I can bring over. Late dinner?"

"Sure. I'll cook."

And just like that, I've made a friend. Gotta say, it feels good.

5

C hapter Five

SOFIA

The sun is just starting to set and the rays still cast a warm, glow over the city streets of Artsbridge. Sunset is the perfect backdrop for the Blue Ridge Mountains, showing off the splendor of Mother Nature.

The cottages are not far and most days I look forward to the walk home because it gives me time to think and wind down, but not this time.

This time I'm walking alongside a man who just days ago, was my aloof, grumpy, possibly serial killer in hiding, neighbor. Now he's a man who has the power to make my body surge with untapped sexual desire just by one glance from those amazing, mesmerizing brown eyes.

He's doing that thing now. Talking and pointing out something and then turning that gaze on me as if I am the only living thing on the planet.

"What did you say?" I say stupidly. I have no clue what he said. I'm too busy trying to remember if I've ever seen eyes quite like his with those small flecks of gold coloring.

Jack laughs. "I said, "How do you get around in the winter time? You don't have a car."

"I don't have one now. My Tio Carlos let me borrow one of his when I first came here almost two years ago."

"Wrecked it?"

"No." I don't want to tell Jack that last year Uncle Carlos took back his car, and later I found out he used it to pay off a gambling debt, leaving me with no transportation. Good thing the bakery was within walking distance, which is probably why I never bothered to buy another one. I shrug. "I don't really need one, and if I really did, Bailey lets me borrow hers. Works for me."

"If you say so," Jack says easily enough, but there's something in the tone that lets me know he's filed that away for a future conversation.

We walk up the cobblestone pathway towards the run-down, 1960s era cottages and then we arrive at the part where the path branches into two paths leading to either cottage.

"I'll be right over with the steaks," Jack says.

"And I'll be right here with the wine," I say with a grin and exaggerated hand flourish towards my place.

I open my door, step inside and lean against the closed door for a second. "Sofia girl, just what are you doing? I mutter aloud. I look around my little place and note with satisfaction that everything is neat and clean.

I love my eclectic décor. It's fun and colorful and overall, very much shabby chic.

My easel is in the corner, looking somewhat abandoned. I haven't had time to finish the work in progress currently on the easel, but I do have some finished pieces from my portfolio that I can show Jack.

I walk over to the small area I call my artist's corner and begin pulling out a few pieces. I handle each one carefully, like they are old friends that I can talk to. I smile slightly when I see an early piece. It was a picture of Drago, our family dog for many, many years. There's an older piece I did of an old woman in the market place and then there's my favorite: a portrait of my mother on her wedding day. The face that stares out at me is young, with eyes full of reverent hope and beauty.

Tears of loneliness threaten to spring up but the pity train stops in its tracks at the sound of a knock at the door. It's gotta be Jack.

I go and open the door. Jack is standing there with a bag and two wine glasses.

He's no longer wearing the white linen blazer and nice slacks. He's exchanged those for a black t-shirt that shows off his muscular chest and tanned arms in a perfectly attractive manner. *Damn, this man is fine and he'd look even finer with a little less scruff on his face and with his hair cut and styled.*

I throw open the door, wide. "Come in. You know I do have glasses, too," I add as he walks past.

Jack shrugs. "Just in case."

"If those are the steaks, I'll take them."

Jack hands me the bag and I take them into the kitchen to prepare them for my indoor grill.

A second later I pop back out. "Red or white wine?"

"Red."

"Shiraz it is."

"Or beer?" he asks with a hopeful expression.

"Hmm, no sorry. Fresh out of beer," I smirk. "I've got ice tea, seltzer water—the non-bougie kind—"

Jack returns the smirk. "I'll have the non-bougie water along with my red, please."

I get Jack set up with a cold can of seltzer water, a glass of red, and a coaster. Then I return to the kitchen to put the steaks on, and place two baked potatoes into the microwave oven. While the potatoes are cooking, I whip out the fixings for a salad, and in no time, the kitchen fills with the succulent aroma of seasoned steaks cooking and I have the makings of a quick, decent meal.

When everything's ready, I lay out the dinnerware I so rarely use. I'm a paper plate and plastic utensils kinda gal so this is what passes for formal dining in my little run-down cottage.

I'm glad Jack doesn't seem bothered by it as he takes a seat at the table as if he belongs there and always has.

He takes a bite of steak, chews and swallows.

I wait, just taking in the sight of this handsome man, sitting across from me.

"Tastes wonderful." His compliment sounds sincere, and his light brown eyes with the gold flecks are liquid pools of sensual invitation.

It is Jack with his adorable, scruffy look, not quite hiding those chiseled features who looks wonderful and tasty. I want to be the napkin that he's stroking across his lips. I mentally shake my head. *I'm happy to be friends. Why the hell did I say that? Friends with benefits is more like it...*

All through the rest of the meal, we keep the conversation light and easy. We banter back and forth and I give as good as I get. Then, when the last bite of food is gone, it's time to show Jack my art and see what he thinks.

Suddenly, my ease around Jack drops off a cliff and I'm filled with nervousness. What if he tells me I have no talent and not to quit my day job? Well, that would suck, but I guess I'd have to re-evaluate my ambitions.

"So...can I show you some of my art?"

"I'd love to take a look."

We walk over to my tiny art corner and I pull the cloth back from the finished pieces I pulled out. The painting of Drago the family dog is the one Jack examines first. My stomach has suddenly grown butterflies in flight and I'm watching as he silently moves to intensely examine a different painting.

"Wh.."?

"Shh..." Jack interrupts before I can finish asking what he thought of the first two paintings.

I rein in my urge to demand a verdict.

One by one, he looks at each of my offerings, including the long unfinished one on the easel. Finally, he looks up at me and his eyes linger on my face. "You are talented, Sofia."

"Really?" Oh my God, I sound like a gushing schoolgirl, not the confident, take-charge woman that I am.

"Really. See this?" Jack is gesturing to the portrait of the old man. "Your brushwork demonstrates confidence. You've captured his essence very well. I can see the stories hidden in his eyes."

"Thank you." I'm proud of how neutral my voice sounds.

"But.." he continues, "here lies your challenge. The texture of his skin—it's raw, visceral. But don't shy away from imperfections. Embrace them." Jack indicates the subject's furrowed brow, and the creases around his mouth. "Allow the light to carve his features."

Jack moves to the next canvas, leaning in close to point alongside the delicate strokes forming the crease of her smile. It's the portrait of my mother. He has no clue of just how much that painting means to me.

"Here. Don't be afraid to push the shadows deeper along her cheekbones. That will really bring out the hope her eyes speak of."

I can't help but nod. I'm thrilled. Jack's critiques are enlightening and spot-on. "That's my mother on her wedding day," I whisper.

"Yes, I know. She's beautiful. You look so much like her. Well done," Jack replies softly.

I watch as Jack picks up the painting of Drago— my family dog forever immortalized on canvas. I remember how I struggled to capture a more natural, breathing presence.

"Your color palette is so ethereal. Look closer here. Jack's finger traces the left side of Drago's face. "The edges should be more subtly blended. This allows the transitions to breathe a little, you understand?"

"Yes. Yes, I see that." And I do. Jack has no idea how much his words are like keys that are unlocking doors I hadn't known were locked.

Finally, Jack turns his attention to my unfinished work on the easel. "Sofia, talent is the spark and technique, a chisel. But the result—the emotion you evoke—that's the alchemy. Keep pushing. Your portraits breathe; they pulse with life."

Jack was incredible. He didn't hold back on ways to improve but assured me that improvement comes with experience and that my work definitely had potential. I know he wasn't just saying stuff so that my feelings wouldn't be hurt.

"Thank you, Jack. I really appreciate you coming over to take a look at my art." I'm reluctant to end the evening, but I walk with him towards the door.

"I was glad to." Jack rests his hand lightly on my arm and the feeling is instant. It's warm electricity tingling up my arm, making a bee-line to my feminine parts. My eyes go wide.

"I mean it, Sofia. You have talent. Don't stop painting."

If Jack is feeling something too, he's being a gentleman and his anatomy isn't betraying him either. When he reaches the door, he opens it, but stops briefly and he looks as though he's debating with himself about something. He runs a hand through his thick hair and turns those gorgeous eyes on me when he speaks what's on his mind.

"Would you like to go with me to visit some art exhibitions this weekend?

The smile on my face isn't as big as the one in my heart. *You bet I would.*

6

∞ ▮ ∞

Chapter Six

JULIAN

Two nights later, Miriam appears at my door, grey hair cut in a stylish short bob. She is impeccably dressed, and her usual self-assured grin is in place. I usher her into the chaos of my studio, where she looks oddly at home among the scattered paint tubes and unfinished canvases.

"So, Sofia," she begins, easing herself onto a stool. "Took a bit of digging, but I found her. Sofia Fernandez runs the place with her uncle. Her father's brother. She moved here from Buenos Aires, Argentina. Has dreams bigger than that bakery by all accounts."

"She's an artist. A good one—with the right polishing and experience," I add.

"You already know? Don't tell me..."

"Nothing happened. We had a late dinner on Saturday night, next door, and then we took in some art at various places. She is one very awesome person. She has a most unique outlook on life. Nothing seems to dampen her zest."

"She's got a family back in Argentina she's supporting, sending money back regularly. Her uncle, a man by the name of Carlos Fernandez, is her sponsor. He hangs with the high rollers but he has zero money or assets apart from that bakery, which he's almost lost more than once," Miriam adds, watching me closely. "I'd be absolutely certain she hasn't worked out who you are and is looking for money."

I shake my head. "No. She's not that person, I'm sure."

Miriam shrugs. "They never are but you need to be sure."

"I'm not marrying the lady. You are the one who told me to get some friends."

"I know. I'm just being ultra-cautious. You've been here six months, it's not hard to imagine that she might have found your true identity and is exploiting that."

"I don't care, Miriam." My voice is cold, and suddenly, I'm fortifying my defenses against a crack in the door of old hurt. "Even if she has. Why does it matter? I can choose who I give money to."

I lock gazes with Miriam while an awkward silence brews between us. "Is there anything else you found out?" I ask, abruptly ending the stalemate.

"There's more. She's signed up for the model auction for the Artsbridge Charity Art Gala month as a late entry. The auction is happening the weekend after next. Seems like a coincidence," Miriam continues, raising an eyebrow. "Could prove that she's looking for fast money."

The news hits me like a bucket of ice water. Sofia hadn't mentioned the auction entry to me. I don't know why. No matter. "It proves she's trying to cut herself a break in the art world. You know this is the month that in previous years, almost all of the best new talent in modeling and art have been discovered. That's why I always support the Artsbridge Charity Gala."

"I'm going to buy her and paint her portrait. I'll bid anonymously. No one can know it's me," I say abruptly, the decision crystalizes because I can't shake the extreme distaste I feel at the thought of someone else having her naked like that.

Miriam frowns. "But you know the art is sold for charity. Your work will be immediately recognized. So you'll have to come clean, at least with Sofia. The media hounds will be back to searching relentlessly for a scoop."

"I'll buy the work as well. Her chosen charity can get the money. No one has to know what the painting even looks like. It will be put in my private collection. You can be a talent scout who buys her for me, an up-and-coming abstract artist to paint." I run the options through my brain, it all seems to make sense to me.

Miriam shakes her head. "That won't work. You know the rules are strict. The artist must purchase the model. Something about their muse or some crap. And the work must go public for sale."

"I'm buying her. You work out the rest. I'll do two paintings if I have to. One abstract to sell. I don't care how it works out. Use whatever money you need to."

Miriam shakes her head. "For someone walking away from his entitled life, you are sure sounding very entitled right now. I'll set it up. But Julian, what's this really about? Are you ready to paint portraits again?"

"It's... a one-time deal," I cut in, unsure how to explain the restlessness that's taken hold, the need to capture something raw and untamed on canvas. Something I'd seen in Sofia's eyes. Something I'd felt deep in my core. If I can't possess her because I'm too broken for relationships, I can capture her on a canvas. "Nothing else has changed."

Chapter Seven

SOFIA

It's auction night! The first Friday night of Artsbridge Charity Arts Gala month is finally here. It's four weeks of everything local and semi-international that is art and a real chance for me to kickstart my successful entry into the art world.

The Commodore is a two-hundred-year-old theater in the heart of downtown Artsbridge. It's an elegant building with heavy red velvet drapes and beautifully polished dark wood paneling and trim. There are rows and rows of plush seating while above there is a balcony and alcove seating.

It's the perfect venue for this vibrant, exciting event. Still functional, it's hosted many productions, exhibitions and performing artists over the years.

For the thousandth time I check the website for the full nude artist model auction requirements, making sure I understand what's going to happen. Everyone who signed up to participate in the auction was urged to read the requirements beforehand. That includes the requirement to have a two-piece swimsuit to wear for women, and swim briefs for men.

There are eleven of us, unsurprisingly, more women than men. It's an interesting mix of people. Most are close to my age, with a handful of middle-aged men and women, and one man old enough to be my granddad.

I'm reminded that this is for art and that a good artist develops the skills necessary to draw the human body no matter how it appears. There's nothing sexual about it and that's a fact I find comforting...especially after the deep unhappiness of Uncle Tio when he found out about my plans to participate in the Artsbridge Charity Art Gala nude art model auction:

"You're going to do what? No! No! No! Sofia, you are not going to take your clothes off in public like some...some strumpet!" Uncle Carlos states vehemently when I tell him my plan to save the bakery.

"Some what? I don't know that word, but the implication is annoyingly clear. Tio Carlos loves me, but he's old fashioned. I had to make him understand what a nude model artist does.

"Listen to me, Tio. Do you even know what a nude artist model does?"

"Whatever they do, it is not how my brother's child will save my bakery."

"Good nude art models are professional. It's hard work. You have to be able to sit still for long periods of time and take direction. There's nothing sexual about it and I'm going to do this whether you want me to or not."

"I don't like it. What will your father say?"

He has me there. Old fashioned and stubborn are qualities these two brothers share. My father would have a lot to say about it...and none of it good.

"He will say that I am a work of art like Michelangelo's David," I lie softly. "It's not just about you and the bakery. It's about me, and maybe the chance to get into the art world a lot faster than I ever could without it. Besides, you know how prestigious an event the Artsbridge Charity Art

Gala is. Famous artists and wealthy people from around the world come to little ole Artsbridge just to participate. Do you really think they would be involved in anything scandalous?"

Tio stares at me hard, thinking.

I have a reprieve when his shoulders sag and he sighs in resignation.

"You're not a little girl anymore, Sofia. Do what you think is best."

"Twenty minutes until show time! Is everybody ready?" Amelia Foster, a matron of the community and one of the key coordinators cheerfully calls out, snapping me back to the present. This woman is everywhere like a hummingbird in fast-moving flight, clipboard in hand and wearing an earpiece for communication. From the get-go she's orchestrating the model hopefuls, showing us to the dressing rooms and going over the process.

My stomach churns even though I have a whole support crowd out there. Bailey is backstage with me for moral support as we wait alongside the other nude model hopefuls.

Bailey gently grabs my arm and steers me towards the dressing area. "Go," she says. "Better get changed now."

"Okay." I move to one of the dressing rooms designated for women and I find a place to disrobe and put on my swimsuit.

After I'm dressed, I take a moment to look at myself in the large vanity mirror with the bright lights around it. I'm not vain but I like what I see. Slim waist, flat stomach, firm arms, thighs and full, generous breasts. My rear end is shapely and fills out the suit bottoms nicely. I nod my head and give a little salute before heading back out.

When I emerge from the dressing room, Bailey is there. She looks me up and down and whistles softly in amusement. "I think I'm jealous," she jokes.

"Not too late to enter," I quip back.

But it's me who is about to step under the stage lights in the hope there's more than one artist who wants to buy me as a model for the charity auction.

I was grateful for the way Jack indirectly convinced me I could do this when we had dinner in my cottage almost two weeks ago and he appraised my paintings. I hadn't mentioned I was entering the auction, but his feedback about my art had been honest and not all bad, making me dare to hope that there is a path for me to sell my art.

Since then we'd visited every exhibition we could in the surrounding area and been to some private showings in homes. It's really kickstarted my creative juices. Okay, maybe some of the juices are not just creative. But, we hadn't gotten anywhere near kissing again. We'd laughed hard, been overly judgy about other people's art, and generally had such a great time.

I have a lot of friends but being with someone who gets the art thing is so good and so easy. He'd been the perfect friend. Not overstepping any boundaries. I'd learned more about my art in the past two weeks than my entire adult life. I can't believe how much Jack took an interest in my work, yet I can't deny my physical attraction to him. It goes against everything I said to him, I want him to be my first.

I must be crazy.

Now, Bailey and I are elbow-deep in a sea of modeling hopefuls backstage. The art-model auction is buzzing with electric excitement and the loud music with the upbeat tempo is stirring up the feelings. We're both jittery with nerves, our hands clasped together for moral support. I feel so at home in this dynamic atmosphere.

"This is it, Sof. Big money, come on!" Bailey whispers, her eyes sparkling with a mix of hope and mischief.

I can't help but laugh, her enthusiasm infectious despite the butterflies doing kung-fu in my stomach over this auction. What if it's a big flop? "Let's not jinx it. I'll be happy with enough money to keep the lights on at the bakery," I say, trying to keep my expectations in check. I'm not lying though.

But as I'm ushered onto the stage by the crew, something shifts in the air—a tangible sense of anticipation that makes my skin tingle. I feel eyes on me and I don't hate it. The curtain is still closed so the crew uses flashlights to illuminate the floor so we can all find our numbers on the floor and stand in our assigned places.

From beyond the curtain, I hear the booming disembodied voice of the Master of Ceremonies. "Ladies and Gentlemen, it's time for one of the most highly anticipated events for the 17th annual, Artsbridge Charity Art Gala—the nude art model auction.

The place breaks out in wild applause, raucous cheers and whistles that seem to go on for a long time. It's contagious and I can't help but smile and clap too, although no one can see me.

The MC is saying something else, but what I don't know because the curtain is lifting and all of us shrouded in darkness are now bathed in our own spotlights that shine down on us to create a circle on the floor.

Despite the overwhelming crowd enthusiasm, there is still a sense of order that underlies the serious intent of this event. One by one we are introduced and urged to turn a complete circle.

I strike a pose with my hands on my hips, drop the smile from my face, and lower my eyelids slightly.

Some very loud cheering happens in one section of the room and despite the bright stage lights in my eyes, I see my bakery regulars all together in the front row, clapping and urging me on. Bailey is right, I am a part of this community. I love the feeling of belonging. I study the crowd a little more, disappointed Jack isn't out there peering back at me.

Finally, the auctioneer kicks things off with a flourish, and bids start flying. I have to say being bid upon is a little weird, but I remind myself it's for a great cause and the family bakery. Bailey cheering from the side of the stage blends with the increasing noise of the crowd as the bids rise.

The energy propels me into a surreal state of hope. I mean, there is obviously more than one person who wants me to sit for them. Quite a few, it seems, and before long the bids have gone into the thousands. I'm actually stunned.

Then, out of nowhere, the auctioneer announces a staggering bid, halting any further competition. "Online bid. Two hundred and fifty thousand dollars! It's a record, folks! Sofia Fernandez is a record breaker." The room falls silent, then erupts into bedlam with cheers and whistles.

It's beyond anything I dared dream. I'm speechless, a rush of emotions flooding me all at once. My eyes prickle with tears and I clasp my hands behind my back, so no one sees them shaking. One hundred and twenty-five thousand dollars for the bakery. That is amazing.

"Who in the world?" I gasp as I step backstage again, Bailey practically tackles with a bear hug.

"Girl, you just hit the jackpot! No, wait, you *are* the jackpot!" she exclaims, her excitement bouncing off the walls as I head back to the dressing room to put my street clothes back on. "What a way to spend Friday night!"

Once redressed, the whirlwind doesn't stop there. Amidst a flurry of activity, I'm introduced to the concept of privacy agreements, the logistics of the portrait sessions and the persistence of clicking cameras.

One of my regular customers, Enid Green, is a respected attorney. I see her now serving as an official behind the contracts desk.

Enid waves me over and indicates the chair across from her desk. Her tight bun is in place as always and her navy-blue skirt suit looks impeccable. Someone said she's eighty years old, but I can't see it. Maybe sixty-five. Hard to tell with her darker skin tone.

"Multiple portrait sitting sessions, all discreet," she says as she flicks through some papers. "Read this contract and come back with any counter suggestions." She hands me stapled papers in a plastic sleeve.

"The winning bidder is open to negotiations," Enid explains, sliding the paperwork across the table. "The initial meeting will be in Washington D.C. next weekend, on Sunday. That gives you time to read these properly. Don't sign anything you aren't comfortable with. Being naked is only ever by your consent, and if at any time you feel uncomfortable or not safe, you can say no. If you're not sure about any part of the contract, here's my card. Call me."

I take the card and slide it in my jeans pocket. My head is spinning with information overload. I need a drink but I have the early Saturday shift tomorrow, so I mustn't overdo it. "This is nothing like I imagined it would be," I admit. But I still can't wipe the smile off my face. My happiness cup is overflowing.

"Protecting yourself is key here, but you can also make the most of opportunities. Find yourself a good manager—someone you trust—and even then, do not take your eyes off your financials. I'm an old girl but I still know a thing or two about the legal side of things." She winks at me. "Congratulations, Sofia. I don't think that record will be broken in a while. Look, there will probably be a media frenzy on this, so be aware."

"Thank you. I will take some time. It's a lot." I smile. "Do you know who the bidder is?"

"No. They want to remain anonymous. Which is fine. I guess you will find out in due course. You've caused quite a stir, young lady."

"It's just so much money, it feels, I dunno, like it's not real."

"You *are* real, don't forget that, and half that money is yours. You choose where it goes. Just in case you were thinking of putting it into your uncle's business, I would advise you not to until you get a formal agreement. Come and see me on that as well. You do nothing but brighten everyone's day and you never hesitate to help those in need. No one deserves this break like you do. Give 'em hell, Sofia."

I give her a big smile and get up to go hug her. "Thanks Enid, I'll sure try. See you in the morning for your usual."

***

The week flew by and I no longer needed to dodge the press and avoid social media as life moved on to the next story. The constant chatter about the auction at the bakery, and the pictures that were posted on the internet had been so crazy. But I knew to ignore them and just get on with my life. Besides, the bakery's future is looking better because once the money clears, I'll be able to pay the debt. Tio Carlos had mentioned again about me running the place. I'm still not sure about that.

I haven't seen Jack since before the auction. He had told me that he had to go out of town for a while. I was dying to tell him all about it and get his ideas on how I maximize this opportunity. Okay, truth is, I was also dying to be close enough to him to watch his lips as my name came out of his mouth.

I miss him being around and we haven't exchanged numbers. I kinda wanted to ask for his but I didn't want to pressure him, so I let it go.

I hope everything is okay with him.

8

C hapter Eight
SOFIA

I'm awakened from a dreamless sleep by the obnoxious blaring of an alarm clock, set too close to my head. The sheets on this bed feel so soft, warm and comfy, and like a child, I pull them up and over my head, determined to snuggle in and ignore the claxon interrupting my sleep.

Wait a minute. This is not my bed with the slightly saggy mattress and old box spring. I'm not in my cottage with the 'vintage' appliances. My eyes spring open and I can see elegant drapes, and five-star hotel furnishings, all paid for by the person who bought me in the auction.

This is not Artsbridge, Maryland. This is Washington D.C. It's that Sunday, and last night, I made the five-hour drive to the District in order to sign papers and meet the artist who had the winning bid at the auction. *Thank you, Bailey for letting me borrow your car.*

Finally, I turn off the alarm and just lie in bed, staring up at the ceiling. My life's been off the charts lately and I have exactly 90 minutes to get out of the door and to an appointment to meet the unknown artist who spent an obscene amount of money for the right to draw my naked body.

At first, I was merely curious about the identity of the artist. Was the artist male? Female? Wealthy for sure—old, most likely. Today my curiosity has grown into nervous butterflies.

I finally get out of bed and head to the spacious bathroom with its ornate fixtures. I'm impressed by the selection of high-end toiletries, and even though I brought my own, I used them all to wash my hair and body in the shower. The shower feels glorious, but I can't linger, so I reluctantly wrap things up.

I cover myself in a big, fluffy, white towel and blow dry my hair. No fancy hairstyle for me. A slicked-back ponytail and light on the make-up is what I decide upon.

I had laid out my outfit the night before and now I quickly put on the forest green, two-piece, knit sweater set, add a fashionable belt as an accessory, and slip on a pair of stylish, low-heeled mules. I have no intention of getting dressed up for this meeting because, clearly, that's not the artist's area of interest in me.

I give myself the once over in the mirror and a mental thumbs up, and then it is time to grab a bite of breakfast before checking out of the hotel.

Once I get to Bailey's car, I double-check the building address before putting it into the GPS. It's not far, but I already know that D.C. is notorious for having street closures and inconvenient, one-way streets that seemingly exist solely to keep people from their destinations. Fortunately, I encounter none of those things, and easily steer the car into a parking garage next to an impressive-looking office building.

When I walk through the center set of glass doors I am nearly overcome by a sense that my life may never be the same.

The elevator doors open and I squeeze in with other riders and get off at the fourth floor. Oh God, have I just passed the point of no return? I want so badly to be a respected artist one day, but I never thought that becoming a nude art model could possibly be my way to achieve that. The answer lies in an office beyond the double wood-carved doors in front of me.

A receptionist ushers me into an office where I'm instructed to sit and wait. I can't sit. I'm too nervous for that.

"Hi, I'm Miriam. Thanks for coming." A small, slim woman in a tailored suit walks in and approaches me with her hand extended towards me. I take it and her handshake is firm, professional, and somehow reassuring in its confidence. "Please, take a seat."

"Are you the artist?" I tilt my head slightly, trying to place her in the puzzle of this unexpected chapter of my life as I sit in the leather chair.

"No. I'm not. I just sign the checks and provide the, well, less financially viable artists with the funding." She sits forward in her chair. "The artist won't be revealed until you sign the NDA."

"Non-disclosure agreement, correct?"

"Correct."

"Why did you bid so much for me? It seems like a ridiculous amount." I bite my lip. This is really unknown territory. Maybe asking that is inappropriate.

"It's not all that much when you consider I have millionaire and billionaire buyers who are always looking for the next big thing. They want in first and they are prepared to add to their collection in the hopes it will pay off later. I represent a lot of models and artists. I have a very talented artist who wants to paint you and I'm betting it will pay off big time."

"But why me?" I frown, self-doubt creeping in despite her encouraging words.

"Look, I don't get into all that artist mumbo jumbo. It's really messy inside their heads. I've discovered some gems, that's all. You might be next, if you play your cards right." She spreads her hands, a gesture meant to encompass the possibilities that lay before me.

"If I get naked, you mean." My arms cross over my chest defensively, the vulnerability of the situation suddenly pressing in. I don't want to feel as though I'm compromising my integrity or morals just to get where I want to be.

"If you have that certain something that artists and designers can work with—and you certainly have a look they'll love—then you can potentially make a name for yourself. But it will come back to hard work and attitude. It's not runway glamor. Ultimately, how you express yourself is up to you."

Her sincerity shines through, making me uncross my arms and consider her words more openly.

"What if I want to be an artist?" My voice is small but determined, clinging to the dream that's at the heart of my aspirations.

Miriam doesn't look surprised by my question. "Now that depends on how your art appeals to the critics and the buyers. There will definitely be a lot of doors open for you if this goes well. No promises, because art appreciation can be fickle, but you'll meet a lot of people who can help you."

That's all I really want to know. Will this get the right doors to open?

I sign the papers and Miriam excuses herself.

My fingers twist at the hem of my shirt, my nervous energy pumping.

"Hello, Sofia." The familiar, baritone smooth voice, unexpectedly here, slices through the silence and makes me freeze.

Then my head snaps up. Jack! Eyes wide, my heart skips a beat. It's really him. Same mesmerizing light brown eyes with flecks of gold. His thick, dirty-blond hair looks like it's seen a comb, but his facial hair hasn't changed. It's really him, standing there, all casual as if his sudden presence shouldn't turn my world upside down. "Jack! What the hell are you doing here?" I can't hide the shock in my voice as I stand up abruptly, my chair scraping loudly against the floor.

"Confession time. I'm the artist." His admission hangs in the air.

"What?" My voice cracks from a mix of shock at his appearance, and happiness to see him. Hell, he could have just asked to paint me for free. But why all the secrecy?

"Do you want to change your mind?" There's a familiar undercurrent of challenge in his question as his light brown eyes search mine for a reaction.

"Not on your life. I mean, it's fine. This is just... unexpected." The ground is still shifting beneath me as I try to reconcile this revelation, but for now I'm determined to play it cool. Later, I most definitely will be trying to find out more about this man who is my next door neighbor.

Jack walks over to me and his body leans close, almost in my personal space. The wood-scent of him is something clean, strong, and masculine. He's looking at me intently. Clearly, there's more he wants to say to me.

"You can't tell anyone I'm the artist. Part of my persona as an abstract artist is not fully revealing who I am. It keeps the mystery. Not even your best friend can know that I'm painting you. I must remain anonymous." His tone is firm, leaving no room for negotiation.

So that's why he's being mysterious.

"I will honor what I signed just now." Honestly, I don't care. I'm here for a chance to save the bakery and make a path to becoming a professional artist. If some crazy recluse artist, who happens to be my sexy neighbor, wants to paint me in the nude, so be it. I can still be his friend.

Too bad the way my body feels right now doesn't have much to do with friendship.

"I need my anonymity protected in a contract, and I really wanted to make sure you were okay with me painting you nude, before you agreed to it all. Miriam got you to sign first, but I'm happy to tear up that contract if you aren't comfortable." He's all business now, but there's a softness in his eyes that wasn't there before.

"Are you running from the law or something?" The question slips out, half-joking, half-serious, as I search his face for clues to the puzzle he presents. "I mean, it does seem strange. You realize that, don't you?"

He shakes his head, a ghost of a smile playing on his lips. "Not running from the law. Sofia, it's a long story. One I hope to share with you one day. For now, I'm asking for your trust as a friend and giving you mine."

Damn. This man is damaged but aren't we all? Everyone needs a friend they can trust. "Trust in the form of a signed contract?" I could kick myself the moment the cynical-sounding words come out of my mouth.

"That is a prerequisite of the Artsbridge Charity Gala," he says flatly.

Ouch. "This is just a friend painting a friend, right?"

"Right. I will promise to do my best so your charity gets the highest amount possible. There was a lot of interest in you as a model, Sofia. Doors will open for you after this."

"Yeah, me in abstract is sure to set the world on fire," I joke.

He grins. "You'd look good in any form."

The little bit of tension that had grown in the room suddenly dissipates.

"I guess you have to prove that now."

"I'd like the first session to start tomorrow night at my studio at the cottage. It won't be late. You have work I know. Then we can work around your schedule. Does that suit?" His offer is casual, as if we're discussing something as mundane as the weather, not the seismic shift in my world of opportunities.

"Tomorrow? Sure. I have no other plans." May as well start as soon as possible.

"You only remove your clothes if that's what you really want, when you're ready. I won't force you. It's an option, okay?" His voice is gentle, reassuring.

For a moment, I forget all about contracts and anonymity and just see the man in front of me; a friend. But I'm under no illusions about how attracted to him I am. I'm a virgin whose vagina is telling me that this is the man to give it up to. I just signed a contract that puts us alone in a room, with me naked, multiple times.

I don't really know how he feels, but I'm not sure my self-control stretches that far.

***

"Finally, you're here." Bailey says as I walk in through the back entrance to the bakery for the early shift the next day.

"Oh sorry, you didn't say you needed your car early today." I apologize as I look around the production area and see Eddie, Jordan and Ava looking expectantly at me and even Gus is suspiciously close to the conversation as he forms dough into the bread tins.

"Spill the tea," Eddie orders with a grin.

"Right now," Jordan says, tattooed arms crossed.

"Oh my God! I'm soooo excited to hear how it went, Sofia. A five star hotel. One of D.C.'s finest. Oh the memories!" Ava spins around and hugs herself.

"I don't care about the stupid car. Why weren't you answering your phone or any of the hundred messages I sent?" Bailey glares at me.

I'd switched my phone off yesterday. So much to think about and I didn't need any distractions. "I needed some time to process." I'm still processing, to be honest. "Really? You're all here just to get the gossip? I wish I'd known that's all it takes to get you lot in here early."

I smile at the variety of faces pulled and I hear Gus give a quiet chuckle.

Eddie brings me over a stool at the other benchtop. "Come on, you know it's killing us. What is the artist like?"

They all sit on a stool at the bench. I sigh and take a seat. They are not going to like my answer. "Look. I signed a non-disclosure. I can't say who it is. Can't say much of anything really. I can confirm the hotel and room was divine though."

"Arrrrrrgh!" Ava fake screams. "I knew it!"

"Don't worry, I swiped all the guest amenities I could and brought them back for you, Ava."

"You are an angel!"

"Surely you can tell us. I mean, we know everything about each other." Eddie begs with wide eyes.

"Rules are made for breaking." Jordan says in agreement.

"I know you didn't just refuse to tell *me*," Bailey says with a shake of her head.

Normally, I probably would have broken the rules for them but seeing as it's Jack and he needs my loyalty on this one, I know I can't even though I'm practically bursting to tell someone. "Sorry but this is about more than just this painting. This is about the rest of my life and my dreams. I'm not going to ruin that chance. I hope you all understand."

Eddie pouts and Jordan says, "damn!"

Bailey stares at me like I'm headless or something. "But—" she starts before Gus interjects.

"That's it. Sofia isn't able to say any more and as her friends and workmates you need to support her on this." He turns around and takes a couple of steps over to us. "It's fine. When you can tell us more, you do that. For now, we're here for you." He wipes his big hand on his apron and squeezes my shoulder. I appreciate this man so much.

"You're right, Gus. Sorry Sofia, we're all just so excited for you," Jordan explains.

"Yeah, babe. You deserve all the good stuff." Eddie places his hand over mine.

"I've already heard all I need to know. I'll go turn on the coffee machine." Ava says with a wide smile as she stands and kisses my cheek. "If you need anything, I mean with fashion tips or hair and makeup, don't hesitate to ask me."

"Considering my idea of style is a scrunchie and clear lip gloss, I may be calling you soon."

They all move off to do their work and I'm left here with Bailey and I look at her. "I am almost splitting at the seams to tell someone. I think I will die if I can't tell you, Bailey."

"Surely there's a loophole. Can't you just ask the artist if you can tell one other person that you trust."

"I'm going to ask, for sure. The first session is tonight, and I'm so nervous."

9

·····•·····

Chapter Nine

JULIAN

Sofia looks around my cottage with its small, but functional studio, her gorgeous eyes wide with a mixture of curiosity and awe. "So, this is your place. I like it. Suits you."

"Dark and messy?" I can't help but grin at her, leaning back against the edge of the worktable to watch her reaction.

"You said it. Not me. But there, you smiled. Now I have hope." Her gaze meets mine, sparkling with challenge and something attractively warm, soft, and inviting.

"Are you sure you're okay with this?" I stand up straight, strongly wanting to keep any awkwardness from growing between us. "I mean, if you don't want to be naked I can adjust the contract."

"I haven't told anyone where I am or who I'm with, just that I'm at the first session tonight," she waves her cell phone. Her voice is steady, but her hands gripping the phone betray a possible nervousness. "But, speaking of changing the contract, I was going to ask if I can just confide in Bailey. I know I can completely trust her and this might change my whole life. I need to talk to somebody for support."

I can't help my initial gut reaction. I take a step back and turn away from Sofia to hide my expression. Memories of betrayal, loss of privacy arise like ghostly specters. I feel suspicion of Sofia and her motives for so easily agreeing to protect my identity in a contract, then so quickly wanting to break it.

I hate this feeling. Something needs to change. *I* need to change. I slowly turn around and look into Sofia's beautiful face. Her eyes are guileless, wide and waiting patiently for my verdict. Looking at her I suddenly realize I'd honestly agree to let her tell the whole world if it made her happy. "Just Bailey? Are you sure?"

She nods. "Absolutely."

"I'm sure the bakery crew would all love to know that you may be getting naked with your grumpy husband tonight."

She flushes a deep, delightful shade of red. "Shit, you know about that?"

"I worked it out, yes. I think it's funny." I take a deep breath. I'm going all in. "You can tell Bailey, provided she signs an NDA first."

"Thank you." She smiles, temporarily derailing any hint of growing tension. I watch as she walks up to my work in progress on the other easel. The way she moves always seems fluid and seductive. She eyes the painting carefully as she speaks. "So, how do we do this? I mean I'm just used to a brightly lit room full of art students."

"This session is about laying the base down and working up the outline. There's a robe in the bathroom, you can put that on." I point towards the small adjoining room, fighting the urge to follow her, to close the gap that feels both too wide and not nearly wide enough. "Then we can work on poses. When you feel comfortable, *if* you feel comfortable, you remove the robe."

Her chuckle is light, but not quite enough to hide genuine nervousness. "Okay. I can work with that. I want to do the best for my charity."

"I think with a nude painting of you, I will be able to name my price."

She looks at me with a disbelieving expression before her focus goes back to my painting. "Will I get to see your process?"

"The finished product; not each session." My words are a feeble attempt to maintain some professionalism, but my gaze lingers on her, tracing the lines of her figure as if I could capture her essence with my eyes alone.

She nods. "That would be great. Maybe I can paint you sometime."

"I'd be happy to do some mentor process sessions with you when we're done with this... if you have time."

She laughs. "I'm certain I'll have time. That would be amazing. Thanks." She's staring hard at each of my works now. "Wait! *You're* the mystery abstract artist keeping everyone guessing right now? I saw some of these style abstracts in a show last year."

"You don't miss much, do you? They seem to be getting more popular. Gets me enough to eat for now anyway." I try to inject some levity into the conversation, desperate to distract myself from the urge to reach out and touch her.

"From what I saw, your work is super popular. You've got something special."

Her compliment hits me harder than expected, a flicker of pride warms me from the inside out.

"But you don't sign your work as Jack," she states with one eyebrow raised. "It was, ahhh, initials... MB if I remember correctly."

My mother's initials. Sofia's got a mind like a steel trap and I really need to steer the conversation away from me. "Correct. Maybe modeling will surprise you and be your thing."

"I'd love to be a successful artist. Just do what I truly love and earn a living from it. That's my dream. But I wouldn't knock back modeling if it helps get me where I want to be."

"I know you can certainly make it in modeling, but it may dampen your positivity a bit. There's a lot of superficial people out there in that profession and a lot of shattered dreams."

"No way will it affect me. There's always a silver lining. Anyway, I'm used to superficial. My father and *Tío* Carlos have made it their life mission to hook me up with literally any wealthy man they know. Apparently, that's the only way I can make them proud. The only way any female child can make them proud apparently." She rolls her eyes. "Whatever. I'll prove them wrong. These old stereotypes need to be shifted. I don't have to be ashamed of my naked body."

I clear my throat, suddenly aware of how close she is to me, not hard in this tiny one-bedroom cottage. "We should get started. I've got some poses in mind, but feel free to suggest anything you're comfortable with."

"I'll go get changed."

I wait nervously for her return. I'm not sure I can handle her naked. Maybe I'll tell her to leave the robe on this time. She walks back out in the blue silk robe tied at the middle. "You call the shots in all aspects. Don't worry about taking the robe off this session. It's not necessary."

"How do you want me to stand? This is so awkward." She gives a small smile.

Getting intimate with her is probably the worst thing I can do right now. Getting close means I will have to tell her the truth about who I am eventually. And I would have to risk my heart. Being hurt is never on my agenda again.

I adjust her pose, careful to be respectful, the air between us crackles with unspoken tension. "Don't forget to breathe and have your face to the light for this first session. If you can just loosen the top of the robe down around your shoulders, that will be fine."

"Like this?" she asks, tilting her head, her slightly parted lips glistening, her gaze meeting mine as the robe slips down to reveal perfectly sculpted shoulders. The nape of her neck is begging to be nuzzled. She's so perfect.

"Yeah, just like that," I reply, my voice barely a whisper as I brush her hair off her shoulder and appreciate the perfection of her collarbone. The proximity is maddening, every instinct screaming at me to press the warmth of her skin against mine. I walk back behind my easel and turn around.

She lets the robe drop and it pools around her feet. That was unexpected. She's stunning. Her skin so smooth, her hair cascading around her shoulders, her full, rounded breasts in tightened peaks. My desire hits the roof and I stare at the canvas, struggling to compose myself. The light and shade plays off her glistening skin. Sofia Fernandez is everything I imagine perfection to be. She is humanity incarnate. I intend to show all of what I see in her. I fight my increasing desire, forcing myself to see her from an artist's perspective.

Finally, I'm focusing on the brushstrokes as I create the first of many layers, the lines and curves, shade and light, that will culminate into the final portrait. Not just the paint that will be layered, I want to capture the essence of her. The brightness she shows and the darkness she hides.

Studying her is an exercise in restraint, every stroke a battle between desire and professionalism. I'm forced to be mesmerized by every detail of her outline because the final work rests on getting the foundations right.

"Should I talk?" Sofia begins, breaking the silence.

"I prefer to work in silence. But if it eases your nerves, go ahead. Grab the robe again if you need to."

"I'm okay thanks. You really should sign your real name to your paintings."

"I'd rather be defined by my talent, not my name."

She doesn't push, but I can see the questions in her eyes, the curiosity that's as much a part of her as her confidence. I want to capture that as well, in a future session. For now, it's an accurate but not detailed pencil sketch to be transferred to the canvas in charcoal ready to start laying down the details in oil paint. It's been an hour and the outline of her above the navel is done although I'm regretting not capturing all of the subtle flair of her hips and thighs. However, concentrating on her any lower may lead to me losing all concentration for art. "I think we're done here. You can go and get dressed."

"Okay, cool." Sofia scoops up the robe and heads off to the bathroom.

I carefully cover the drawing and move to wash my hands in the kitchen sink. I turn to see her behind me, fully dressed again. She steps in closer to the canvas. I can't let her see it. It's not the abstract I'd said I'd paint.

I move quickly to intervene. "Sorry. No progress peeks, remember?"

She moves away obligingly, looking elsewhere to explore. Her gaze lands on the only family photo I have on my wall. "Is this your family?"

Family, ooof, another topic I'm keen to avoid. Dad constantly reminds me I'm a source of disappointment to the firstborn legacy. Mom is the exact opposite and wants me to just be me. Like I even know who that is. "Yeah, but I don't want to talk about my family if that's okay."

"Fine by me. I should be going anyway. That session was great. I hope it was okay dropping the robe, but I have to be comfortable expressing myself if I'm going to be a model and also as an artist. It seemed like the right move." Her eyes shine at me and I'm almost certain I see desire. My body reacts immediately and instead of walking her to the door, I step in closer and take her hand in mine.

I drink in everything about her from her intoxicating scent, to her lush lips and tempting curves. My mind is in turmoil over this decision I've already made. Mesmerized by the pull she has on me, I almost hope she chooses to leave. I do think painting her will ease this magnetism. I've suppressed the raw artist in me so long by doing these abstracts, it now demands an outlet.

But she doesn't retreat. She laces her long, elegant fingers in my own sturdy ones and pulls me closer to her. Her lips meet mine, igniting something fierce and wild inside me. I hear a groan and realize it came from me. She answers that passion as her mouth opens and her tongue darts against mine then retreats again like it's been burned. I follow gently with my tongue until I find hers again, hesitant and she sucks in a gasp. The heat between us is undeniable and where other women, determined to trap me, would up the stakes immediately, Sofia doesn't.

The kiss remains soft, slow, exploratory and has my heart beating faster than any other kiss ever has. I resist the urge to be more powerful, to command her to do my bidding, to possess her sexually the way I want. At that moment, I feel as though I could kiss her for the rest of my life like that and never be happier.

Her kiss feels like everything I didn't know I was looking for. Finally, Sofia breaks the kiss. I let her retreat and I suck in a breath of my own. Sofia's beautiful face is flushed and though I read desire clearly in her eyes, she apologizes.

"I'm sorry. I should not have done that."

"It was me. I know we said we are friends and we have this contract now. I don't want you to think this has anything to do with either of those things. But, Sofia. I'd be mad not to want you. This is your choice and I promise I won't speak of it again no matter what we choose right now."

She hesitates a moment. "I want to do this, Jack. I need you too, and we are adults. We can do this, just this once only."

Damned if I know how I'm going to resist her again but I sure as hell am not going to refuse her now. Taking her by the hand, I lead her into my bedroom, which thankfully is clean and bright as I always sleep on the couch, and my paintings dry in here needing a dust-free, well-lit environment. The exact opposite of the rest of this cottage.

"You are gorgeous, Sofia." I gently trace my finger over her full bottom lip and she shivers under my touch. She stares at my erection crushed inside my jeans and then she's in my arms again.

Words spill out of her mouth and I have no clue what she's saying but it sounds so goddamn sexy. "I don't speak Spanish, at least, I think it's Spanish."

She nods and laughs. "Sorry. It's hard to express how I feel in English sometimes, so maybe this will help," she says as she backs away and slowly begins peeling off her top to reveal her heavy, rounded breasts, her rosy pink nipples tight.

I kiss her lips and move to suck and caress each nipple in turn. She writhes and groans under my mouth. I look her in the eyes. "Tell me what you want, Sofia."

"I want you to fuck me. Hard." Her face is aflame as she speaks her truth. No woman has ever looked or sounded so beautiful.

Her fingers trace over my cock, soft and gentle through the denim. My hard member throbs inside my jeans under her delicacy. Then she grips me, squeezing my hardness. "Now. Right now." Her fingers fumble at my button and zipper.

I finish the job, stepping out of my jeans and taking off my shirt and underwear while she hastily peels her jeans and panties off.

Her wide eyes take in every part of me from my heaving chest to my throbbing erection.

"Hurry," she demands.

God, I'm going to burst right now If I don't get inside her. "Are you sure?" I grind out.

"I'm so ready for you, Jack."

I slide my fingers along her heat and they come away slick. She is definitely ready. "Jack," she groans and her hips raise. I taste her essence on my fingers and it's like honey on my lips.

Suddenly, we are both lying side by side on the bed, skin to skin, sexual desire a palpable thing between us. Her soft murmurs spur me on. I'm above her now. Her creamy thighs are open and I ignore the urge to taste more of her from the source, or use my tongue and fingers to bring her to screaming orgasm.

"Take me, Jack. Now. Hurry. I want you."

I position the head of my cock at her wet entrance. I push a little and I don't slip inside her as I expected. There's resistance. She must be nervous, I think. "Guide me in, Sofia. You're in charge. Relax, baby. Let me inside you."

Her hand is wrapped around my shaft and the head touches her soaked opening. She arches up a little and gasps out loud as my swollen cock-head nudges inside her wet tightness. She draws in a sharp breath, and the feeling of internal muscles clenching almost makes me lose control.

"Jack," Sofia's lithe body bucks underneath mine. "That feels so good. Fuck me. Please. Don't stop."

I slide my length inside her slowly and sigh deeply with the incredible pleasure. "Ahhhhhh." Sofia's long legs wrap around my hips and then higher as she pushes up onto me.

Slowly, deliberately, I begin my rhythmic pumping in a dance as old as time and Sofia's hips are keeping the beat, rising and falling with each thrust.

"Faster, harder" she breathes the words sexily in my ear and I do as she asks.

Gripping her buttocks, I slam into her, hard, fast, over and over and Sofia cries out for more each time. Then I know I'm past the point of return and I push hard inside her, grinding onto her clit, filling her as deeply as I can, until the moment arrives and her orgasm hits with powerful waves of intense contractions.

"Fuck! Oh fuck!" She is cursing and shuddering as she comes and I swear my cock will be bruised it's squeezed so hard by her.

Everything I have, everything that's inside me, explodes into her beautiful body and together we ride the waves of red-hot passion and physical need together.

My heaving, sweat-soaked body collapses bonelessly on top of hers before rolling to the side. I can't move so I simply bask in the wonderful sensations of my cock twitching and pulsing inside her and watching Sofia's breasts heave up and down.

Finally, I withdraw and roll onto my side. It seems to take all my strength to drape my leg over Sofia's and stroke her face and hair, waiting for my heart rate to slow down.

The sudden realization of not what we've done, but *how* we did it hits me like a ton of bricks. I grow alarmed. "Fuck. Sofia. Shit, no condom. I'm sorry, I am never that careless."

Sofia looks at me with half-hooded eyes and gently strokes my hair. "I'm on birth control. It's fine."

We finally untangle our bodies and Sofia sits up. I watch as she gets up and begins putting on her clothes.

Suddenly I'm faced with the awkwardness of the situation. We agreed that this was a one-time experience and I don't want to embarrass her, but I'm just not sure what to say now and that is not something I ever struggled with in the years before I chose to get married and settle down.

Silence reigns as I slowly get dressed as well.

I can't believe how amazing being with her felt and yet, now it's over. My heart is screaming at me that this can't be over. Panic is beginning to set in. This isn't me, not anymore. I'm not the guy who gets involved, who lets someone in. I can't go through that hurt again. I pull away, my mood shifting like the tide. My emotions are still raw.

A surge of memories hit me, bringing back all the broken relationships. Every single failure brought about because the women never wanted me for me. They wanted the lifestyle, the money and the status.

Just being me was never good enough. Just when I thought I finally found my person, the one who loved me for me, I found her cheating and the divorce process was messy. There was the scandal, and then the tragedy of her death in a speedboat with her lover before the divorce was final. The silent nail in my coffin—an unborn baby whose DNA proved to be mine. I'd lost something I never even knew I wanted.

"You'd better go," I mutter. I can feel the grumpiness settling in like an old friend. This is who I am now and this is who I will remain.

Oh no, Sofia looks upset. "Yes. I'd better. Early shift. I'll see you soon."

"Sofia, I'm not looking for, well ... anything. I like my life of solitude." Fuck. Now this really does feel awkward.

She shrugs. "It's just sex. People do it every day. It's nature. I'm not asking you for a lifelong commitment and I'm a consenting adult. I don't get why it has to be so complicated. But anyway, you do you, Jack. No pressure."

She leaves without another word, the taste and scent of her lingering, a reminder of what I'm trying so desperately to avoid. Sofia Fernandez, with her easy laughter and open mind, has changed the game.

I can't let this happen again. We're just friends. That's all.

10

Chapter Ten
SOFIA

One week later

"Please, you cannot say anything about this to anyone. It's just once." I give an embarrassed giggle. "I mean it Bailey." We're having Sunday cocktails at my cottage. The owner has replaced all the white goods and the fridge has an ice dispenser, so we're making the most of it. "I know he agreed to me telling you that he's the artist but not to the sex part."

"The sex part isn't in the contract, so fair game." She grins at me. "God. Was it amazing? Was it worth it?"

"Yeah. I mean, wow. I'm not sure I can ever top that, you know?" My heart is racing just thinking about how he made me feel. How I think my first will always be my best.

"Oh girl, I know! But you will, one day. You feel okay about it all then?"

"I dunno, I mean, as far as the physical side of it, hell yes, but afterwards he just got all stormy and I left." I finish, a sigh escaping my lips. "Maybe he just wasn't that into me. It's confusing. Maybe I was a little too desperate and read the room wrong."

"I can tell you this much. You either rocked his world so hard he couldn't handle it or he's just an asshole who's into using women." She winks at me. "I feel it's the first one. I mean, you've been seeing a lot of him." She pulls a face and we giggle. "As friends, I mean."

"Honestly, we have the best time together. Always laughing. He's taken me to art exhibitions, and I've learned so much from him. He's very informed and intelligent when it comes to artists and all mediums. He lives for this stuff."

"So, you don't feel he crossed a line by having sex with you? Is it friends with benefits now?"

"No." I shake my head. "I'm not looking to make it a regular thing and clearly neither is he. I wanted him to be my first but I didn't want him to know that. To treat me differently because I'd never done it before. I just wanted real, raw sex, whatever that meant."

"Girl, you could have been the most disappointed woman in the universe. Trust me, some men just never get it."

"I guess I got lucky." I smile. "But I knew it felt right and Mom always said to trust my gut. She was right."

"I can't even mention Mom and sex in the same sentence without feeling awkward. Here you are talking about it to yours like it's the most natural thing in the world."

"It's our culture. We aren't embarrassed by sexuality, but that doesn't mean we all go around having it constantly."

"You probably will now." Bailey laughs out loud.

I shake my head. "I don't think so. I think we really are one and done. I don't want to lose his friendship, or his support with my art, you know? It's important to me."

"Sounds like you've chosen very wisely, and he is lucky to have you in his corner. I should know." Baileys holds up her glass and I clink mine into it. "So, no sittings this weekend?"

I shake my head. "Just weekday evenings now. He's out of town this weekend. Family stuff."

"Oh. Where is his family from?"

"I'm not sure. We haven't really talked about it. He's not into talking about them."

"But you talk about yours to him?"

"Yeah, sure."

"How much do you know about him? Apart from being an artist with a passion for all things art?"

I shrug. "Not much. But it doesn't matter. I don't need to know everything about him."

"Have you ever met any of his other friends?"

"No. I don't think he mixes with anyone here really."

"Doesn't that seem unusual? I mean does he talk about a childhood friend or school? He must have a bestie. Everyone has a bestie."

"I can feel he has a lot of walls up. But I don't mind. We haven't been friends for all that long."

Her hand touches my hand. "But I know you. Don't get your expectations too high. He may disappear as quickly as he turned up one day."

"Maybe. But I want to just enjoy the time we have as friends and leave it at that."

"Or... we can search him up..."

I look at her. "Should we? I mean... I'm not sure."

"If it's on the internet, it's fair game to read. That's what I think anyway. I'm sure there won't be much."

I kinda feel dirty researching Jack online. I mean it's to satisfy my own curiosity. Not like I'm broadcasting it to the world. Just that he's so guarded in his answers to personal questions, it has piqued my curiosity.

"Anything yet?" Bailey asks as sits back down on my sofa with a mojito for us both.

"Not really." I say as I take the glass. "There's some very superficial stuff and a few pictures of his abstracts under the MB signature. Seems no one seems to know what he looks like. Don't you dare tell anyone about this, it goes against the contract terms, if it gets out I could get sued or something." I sip my cocktail.

"I'm not telling anyone. Why would an artist need to hide who they are? It seems very dramatic to me. I can't even imagine anyone caring."

"It's more common than you think in the creative world."

"What's his last name?"

"I'm embarrassed to say I don't know."

"You've joined private parts and you don't even know his surname? You are going to hell."

"Shut up. You've done worse." I smack her in the arm.

"True. Hey, don't you have a signed contract you can look at?"

"Checked already. It's signed MB like his paintings.

"He is one mysterious artist."

On a whim I type 'mysterious artist' into the search engine on my laptop and press enter. A number of hits come through all of varying interest and none that seem to have any connection to Jack or MB. I look at the image thumbnails on the top of the search page.

Billionaire artist goes underground. Those words catch my attention. I click the link. "This is a classic example of why I hate online research, you get sucked into rabbit holes."

"Did you find something?"

"Clickbait on Julian Blackwood."

"Old news, probably."

I look at the story spread over the page. "Yeah, looks like it." I study the picture of his work. "His portrait work is just so unique and striking. He inspired me to finally develop my own portrait work. Then he and any new work just disappeared. I remember his portraits, but I tried not to get caught up in the sensationalism. His process definitely interests me."

"You artists are a little... eccentric. I only knew him as an attorney with one of the most powerful families in Washington. I mean, what's to complain about? *Oh, I'm so sick and tired of waking up rich. See ya bitches, I'm off to be poor.*" Bailey feigns a dramatic voice and gestures.

"A painting of his sold for five million at auction last year."

"Now that is an artist income we could get used to."

"In my dreams. I'd be lucky to get five bucks in a garage sale for my stuff right now."

"I love your stuff. It's excellent."

"You hate art. What would you know?" I laugh. "Thanks for the support but it's missing a certain something, trust me."

"Maybe it's just missing life experience, heartbreak, pain, and blinding orgasms." Bailey grins.

I grin back. "Well, I got the last one covered. At least once, anyway."

"I'm so jealous. I remember that kind of hard, hot sex from before Rob started medical residency. Now that he's in the middle of it and working such insanely long hours, it's already been a long time since I felt that we had *that* kind of spark. I've been thinking that we need to spice things up a little before we officially tie the knot."

Bailey looks entirely unlike herself with that pensive expression. My heart hurts for her because, clearly, something's wrong and I've been too wrapped up in myself to notice. I reach over and take Bailey's hand. 'Bailey, what's wrong, really?"

Bailey's eyes are suddenly liquid pools of misery. "He loves me so much, but...but I think we probably are meant to just be best friends and not husband and wife."

My heart is breaking for Bailey and I fish for something to say that won't sound trite. "You two have been together for ten years. Any relationship is bound to go through some ups and downs. Maybe all you need is for Rob to finally finish his residency. If not, it's also okay to go find someone who loves you as more than a financial partnership and friend."

"I guess. But it's comfortable, you know."

"I'm sure you'll work it out, Bailey. Stay engaged, get married, or keep single, keep studying and go live the high-life of the excellent surgeon's wife."

"Right alongside my red-carpet-modeling superstar."

We both laugh and clink glasses. "To dreams!" we say in unison.

"I need the bathroom!" Baileys jumps up and runs.

I look back at the page on my laptop and read a little more.

Julian Blackwood says he wants his talent to define him, not his name.

Wait, what? Jack said that exact thing. God is he just copying stuff he reads? I click into the photo, enlarge it. Julian Blackwood, clean-shaven, close-cropped hair with blonde tips on top. I stare at the outline of his face. *Light brown eyes. Are those gold flecks?* I squint and enlarge the image which just results in distorted pixels. I need better images. Now I'm really clutching at straws but I have to prove myself wrong.

Bailey comes back. "I don't think it's good for your eyes getting that close to a computer screen."

"What if Jack is Julian Blackwood?" I blurt out before I can stop myself.

"Are you drunk-joking now, or serious?"

"I'm not sure but there's something about this photo of Julian Blackwood that reminds me of Jack."

An array of images come up and included are some promotional shots with his artwork. I zoom in on his eyes and with better quality images I'm shocked. "I think it actually is, Bailey. His eyes are almost identical."

"The Blackwood men all have the same eyes. Light brown, almost gold. So sexy."

"Well, if this isn't him, he's definitely related." I say and turn my laptop around for her to see the enlarged image.

"No point showing me. I've only seen Jack close that one time when he was limping past me. Can't you use something to make that photo hairier?"

"Bailey, you are a genius! AI can do that for me." I fist bump the air and turn my computer back to me and pull up the webpage. I plug the image into the software and ask it to add scruffy, dark blonde hair and medium-long beard hair. The image is back in seconds. I drink the rest of my mojito straight down. "It's definitely him."

"Stop it."

My heart is hammering right now. I know it's him. I'm not sure what to do with this information. Should I tell him I know? "I swear on my mother's life it's him."

Bailey jumps up and stands behind me to peer over my shoulder. "You wouldn't say that if you weren't convinced."

"You cannot utter a single word. I do not want to be the one who ruins his life again."

"Are you going to tell him you know?"

I shrug. "Do you think it will matter? I mean, we have an art contract. But we're friends, too. I think."

"No wonder you sold for so much. He's into you. You'd never have to worry about money."

"Bailey! You know how I feel about that. I'll make my own way."

My stomach is doing flip flops now. It's not the shock of discovering who he really is, or whether or not he was deceiving me or lying by omission, it's how his real identity changes our relationship and my pursuit of my own art career.

"Jack... Julian, whatever his name is, wants to paint me, but he doesn't want me to know who he really is. Everyone will think that we're a couple when they discover that."

"No wonder he knows so much about art. How can I be friends with him now and have my stuff taken seriously? I'll never know if he hasn't just paid money to get my stuff seen." The words tumble from me.

My mind is full of all the reasons that his billionaire status ruins things for me, but underneath all of that, I feel for him and how hard it must have been to have that laser attention focused on him at such a heartbreaking time of his life.

"I did tell you some people are just assholes."

"It can't have been easy, losing his wife like that and walking away from his family heritage."

"I'm sure he took a few billion with him to survive the heartbreak."

"Bailey, have some empathy."

"I have empathy for Don who's homeless after his house burned down, I have empathy for Ruby who just lost her mom and the grandmother to her kids. Real people we know. Mr. Spoiled Rich Kid throwing a tantrum over having a silver spoon in his mouth, not so much."

"I get your point. But he can't help the family he was born into and clearly, he has hidden pain."

"I swear you would defend a rattle snake if it bit you."

"It would only bite if it felt threatened or had babies to protect."

"There you go!" Bailey sounds exasperated. "You're going to get your heart smashed, Sofia."

"I guess that's a part of life. But I'm not getting in that deep. Once this portrait arrangement is over, I'll tell him what I know. I don't want to interrupt his muse. If he is doing a portrait again, this might be a breakthrough for him."

"And some scorching sex is just a bonus." She smiles again now; she knows me well enough to not try and change my mind any further.

"I'll keep my options open."

Bailey leaves and I'm left reading all the past gossip about Julian Blackwood. Just my luck. The one man I feel a connection with just happens to be exactly what my father expects for me.

I mean, I'm from Argentina, on a visa. What if being connected with Julian Blackwood means the world will assume I'm a gold-digger and just using him as a platform for my art? I couldn't stand that. I want my art to prove itself.

He is everything I need to avoid.

I make up my mind. Once the charity art is done, I'll distance myself and keep his secret. No one will ever take me and my art seriously if they find out my connection to him.

Then there's his family. They can't accept his art. How could they possibly accept me? I'm not telling him I know. I don't want him mentoring me either.

If this wasn't real life, I'd never believe it. Sunday is the next sitting and I need to not end up in his bed. No matter how he makes me feel.

11

Chapter Eleven

JULIAN

"Julian! Darling, you came." My mother rushes up and hugs me.

"Of course, Mom. I'd never miss your birthday."

"Everyone is in the barbeque area. Grab a beer and go say hi. I'm going to bring out some salads."

"I'll help you carry them. The beer can wait."

She lets me out of the hug and taps my cheek. "Still looking scruffy I see. When do I get to see your gorgeous face again?"

"Mom, I'm still me."

"I know, honey. How's your painting going?"

"Okay. I'm getting by."

"Portraits?"

I almost mention Sofia and the auction. Mom has always had my back, encouraging me to follow my dreams. But I definitely do not want her to guess that Sofia and I have any kind of relationship other than professional. So I decide not to mention it. "Still abstracts."

"There's still time, Julian. Just go back to doing what you love. You'll never find anyone while you are living in hiding."

Mom wants me to remarry and be happy. She's convinced my person is still out there. I pick up a slaw and potato salad. "I'm fine,

Mom." I kiss her on the cheek. "Happy birthday. I don't have a gift yet..."

"Having all my boys together is the only gift I need. Come on, let's get these out there and get a drink."

I smile. "Sure." I brace myself for the reaction of my father. I know he always feels more comfortable if I'm not around for these family gatherings but I'm not missing Mom's birthday. He can just get over himself. He has four other sons in the family business. He doesn't need me.

The backyard buzzes with laughter and chatter, the scent of grilled meat fills the air, and there they are—my brothers, all clean-cut, laughing with their wives and kids running around. They're the picture of success and stability, and then there's me, the black sheep, literally and figuratively standing on the outskirts.

I set down the salads on the buffet table and scan for a beer. My youngest brother and the only one who has never been married or engaged, Darien, spots me first. "Julian! Man, you made it!" He claps me on the back, a genuine smile on his face.

"Wouldn't miss it for the world," I reply, trying not to sound sarcastic. I really am happy to be here for Mom.

As I try to blend into the lively scene, my nieces and nephews, a collective whirlwind of energy and giggles, spot me from across the lawn.

"Uncle Julian!" they shriek in unison, launching themselves in my direction. Their small arms wrap around my legs, their faces upturned in pure joy. It's hard not to get swept up in their excitement, to temporarily forget the shadows that linger in my heart.

Each hug, each laugh, is a stark reminder of what's missing in my life—the child I'll never get to know, the future that was stolen before it even began. The betrayal of a woman to whom I'd given my soul.

I tussle their hair, forcing the brightest smile I can muster, all while a part of me aches silently for the might-have-beens.

"Uncle Julian, play with us!" they demand, tugging at my hands and clothes, their energy boundless.

We chase each other around the garden, their shrieks of delight filling the air. I grab some ice from the bucket and shove a cube down each of their tops. They scream and laugh and run in all directions. For a moment, I'm just Uncle Julian, caught up in the pure happiness of the kids. It's a bittersweet reminder of what might have been, the child I lost before even knowing they existed. The weight of that secret grief feels heavier amidst this innocent joy.

Next thing I know, I'm on the ground with three brothers piled up on me and feel the freezing sensation of at least half a bucket of ice cubes down my t-shirt. "Hey, unfair. You ganged up!" I cry out still laughing as I throw each one of them off and stand up, emptying my shirt as I go. "I can still take you all and don't forget, paybacks are a bitch."

"Still delusional, I see." Darien says as he puffs and laughs.

"The only delusion here is the level of fitness you lot think you have," I say with a grin.

"You deserved the ice. We haven't seen you in like, forever," the next eldest James chides, but the warmth in all my brothers' eyes makes me silently promise to make myself more available.

"I'm not into parents breaking sons' balls, but I have to agree with them this time. Can't you at least make that hair presentable?" Brock, the second youngest says. "You look like Grizzly Adams."

We fall into easy banter, the kind that's only possible with those you've known your entire life. For all of our differences, these moments remind me that we're cut from the same cloth. It's a belonging I often forget in my self-imposed isolation. I notice my mother, all smiles as she kisses my father on the cheek. I wonder how she's stayed all these years.

Then Dad's eyes lock onto me. That familiar mix of disappointment and resignation. It's a look I've grown accustomed to, but it still stings. I guess I can't avoid speaking to him forever. Mom would want us to put our differences aside for the day and I'm prepared to do just that for her.

"Julian," he nods, his voice neutral as I get closer and hand him a beer, cracking the lid off my own as well.

"Dad."

"Still in hiding from life I see."

And...here we go. I brace myself for the usual tirade of lectures and begging me to take up what's rightfully mine and stop making our family heritage look like a crock of shit. I swallow half my beer in preparation.

"You're wasting your talent on those abstracts."

I literally choke on my beer. What!? Who is this man and what has he done with my father? I cough and wipe my mouth with a napkin.

I stiffen, ready to defend my choices, but he holds up a hand. "I'm not here to argue about art, Julian. I'm saying, stop running from who you are."

I laugh bitterly. Well, that's a new one for the books. "And who am I, Dad? The failed lawyer? The Blackwood disappointment?"

He shakes his head, a rare moment of vulnerability crossing his face. "You're defining yourself by what you're not, instead of just being. Life's tough, son, but you're tougher. Stop letting the name or the past hold you back."

"You've always seen me as a failure because I didn't want your life," I state my truth.

"That's not true. You made your choices and you never listened to me. Not even once. You knew everything. All I did was try to give you a legacy you could be proud of. But you hated everything about it, everything about me."

Dad thinks I hate everything about him? No. Before I can respond, my mother intervenes. "Charles, we talked about where this conversation should go and I think you're little off track."

Dad's defensiveness seemingly crumbles under her gentle but firm tone. He sighs. "You're right, Lorraine. I need to say what I need to say. Julian, shut up for a second and let me speak."

I step back, my hands in the air. "Knock yourself out." I can't believe this is going to end well but I'm here for it.

"I've been wrong, pushing you into a mold that was never meant for you. I'm sorry, Julian. Your art, your choices... they're yours to make. And they're enough. Except that angry abstract stuff is crap. Go back to what you used to do."

"Wait, you *want* me to paint now?"

He looks at me, something shifting in his gaze. "It's not about the life I want for you, Julian. It's about you running from any life at all because of our name and because of what happened with your marriage. Just be happy. It's all your mother and I really want for all of our boys."

"This is unexpected."

"With all due respect, just stop moping about feeling sorry for yourself. Own your shit. Go take the life you want by the balls and crush the fuck out of it."

"Charles! Language." My mother says but she has a very proud smile on her face. I love seeing her like this.

"Geezus, can you not use balls and crush in the same sentence like that, Dad." I say, effectively showing him I'm no longer wanting any arguments.

He grins back at me. I don't even think I can remember Dad being this happy, ever.

"Dad, are you okay? You're not going to try and die again, are you? Is your heart okay?"

He gives a big belly laugh. *That* I haven't heard for years. "My heart is exactly as it should be. Now we just have to work on yours, son." He wraps his arms around me. A hug! Now I know I'm dreaming.

I want to argue, to tell him he doesn't understand me at all, but his sincerity stops me. Is he right? Have I been so caught up in rebelling against the Blackwood legacy that I've lost sight of what I really need? If he can have a change of heart like that—and I know we still have a long way to go—should I?

I look around my family. We're like any regular family, right? I mean we aren't perfect no matter how much money is in the bank.

Inside the family mansion I stand where Mom has hung the portraits I painted of her and dad on their twentieth anniversary and of my two married brothers and their wives on their wedding days. They're from a time when I poured my soul into my work, unafraid and unapologetic. Looking at them now, I see a part of me that's been buried under layers of resentment and fear.

Is it possible that, in my fight to not be a Blackwood, I've been denying the most essential parts of myself?

I dunno. Maybe it's time to confront those broken pieces, to really examine what I want my life to look like. Sofia's image flashes in my mind, her laughter, her warmth, and for the first time, I wonder if allowing someone in might be part of the solution. She has no clue who I really am, and she seems to like me just fine.

That's what hits me like a ton of bricks. It's not my family background that has me hiding. Not really. That's just been an excuse. It's the thought of ever getting hurt like that again. In the end, even my money and status wasn't enough.

My wife was having an affair with a man who was a tradesman. At the end of the day, it was me she rejected. And later I found out I'd lost a child. I was painting at my best. I was being the best version of myself. I was a happy, loving man who was about to tell his father to take me as I am or not at all.

But I wasn't enough for her. Clearly, she wasn't staying for the money, but even worse, she wasn't staying for me either. I just wasn't enough. I'm not ready to go there again. Keeping things casual is the way to go with Sofia. She seems happy with that, so why rock the boat?

I'm okay. Things seem better with Dad. I'll take that as a win and keep the status quo in my private life. Sofia and I do have something special. I can't deny that, but it's a special friendship. One that can last for a lifetime. This is all the relationship I need.

12

C hapter Twelve
SOFIA

"Sofia I'm selling the bakery!"

"*Tio* Carlos? What?"

"We both know I'll just lose it one day. I'm over trying."

Is he drunk? I've just gotten the money to save the bakery in my bank and I was going to talk to him about part ownership. "*Tio*, I have the money from the auction. You know half of that is for the business."

"I know. I appreciate what you did and if you want to keep running this place, you can. I shouldn't be holding you back. You choose the path you want. You've been good to me, Sofia. It's time you followed your own dreams."

I'm not sure I can believe him. "Did you lose the shop in a bet?"

"No. I promise. I haven't been gambling since we talked last. But, guess what? Beth called and still wanted to see me. I told her the truth. All of it. She doesn't care. Beth wants to travel with me, not be tied to a bakery. We are going back to Argentina for as long as I need."

"Beth?"

"That lady I introduced you to last month. You remember?"

I remember a small lady a little older than him, dripping in diamonds with a happy smile. "Ah, I see. Beth, yes."

"It's not what you think. She isn't rich but she has some assets from her first marriage. She's a widow and a wonderful person. She makes me feel good when we're together. Anyway, the sale goes through at the end of the month. I think your aunt would want me to be happy."

Realization hits me.

"*Tio*. You are my sponsor, and my green card hasn't arrived yet. If I have no job here, what will happen?"

"Sofia, I think it's okay for a short time. I'll find out for you. I'm sorry, but I need to do this. The new owner may want you to stay on if that suits."

Uncle Carlos gently bestows a kiss on my forehead. I read an apology and a plea for understanding in the gesture. This could effectively end my time in the U.S.. But what else can I do? I can't be angry with this man who is so like my father. He deserves to be happy, too.

As I flip the "Closed" sign, a heavy sigh escapes me, and the sting of unshed tears blurs the view. Soon, this will be the last time I do this. The faces of my regulars flash in my mind, as I step away. My heart feels anything but light.

With my world shifting beneath my feet, I dial my mom's number, craving the comfort only she can provide. "*Amá*?"

I start the moment Mom answers, my voice already shaky. "Sofia! How are you, my dear? Your sister Chloe just won a top student award. We're all so proud," she gushes without waiting for my response. Her happiness is a sharp contrast to my turmoil.

"That's fantastic, *Amá*. But, um, can we talk? Just you and me?" My fingers tighten around the phone.

"Of course, sweetheart. What's on your mind?" Her voice softens, ready to catch me, as always.

I swallow hard, the words tasting of defeat. "*Tío* Carlos sold the bakery."

There's a pause, and I can almost see her nodding in understanding, not surprised in the least. When she speaks again, the conversation slides effortlessly from English to Spanish. "Ah, I see. And what will you do now, Sofia?"

The question looms large, and for a moment, I'm a little girl again, unsure and seeking guidance. "I'm not sure, *Amá*. It feels like everything's up in the air. I mean, I have money saved, from the modeling contract. But, I haven't painted in so long..." The admission feels like confessing a sin; my dreams fading like the daylight.

"There's always a place for you here, Sofia. And don't you worry about contracts and commitments. You're more important than any of those things. Just come home. We'll figure it out together," her words, steady and sure, carve a path through my doubts.

I promise to check my contracts, to consider her offer seriously, then it's time to say our goodbyes and end the call.

Funny, there's a lump forming in my throat and I have to fight to get any words out. "Give my sisters a hug from me, especially my favorite, brat, Chloe. And tell *Papí*...well, tell him that I love him."

"Of course, *Mija.*"

"I miss you so much," I whisper, but as I disconnect the call, a sliver of hope flickers in the darkness. Maybe home, with its familiar comforts and unconditional love, is exactly where I need to be to find myself again.

I could afford a nice studio space just outside Buenos Aires for six months. I could put everything into my portraits and have something to show to whom, I don't know. Maybe Miriam? I have some offers for fashion modeling. Surely I can travel from Argentina. At least to start with. But before I get too ahead of myself, I need to talk to Jack, well Julian. I've seen his lights on the past two nights but nothing of him. We also have a contract and a painting to finish for a charity of my choosing.

Half an hour later I tap on his door. No doubt someone's camera is still clicking my every move, but I'm over trying to avoid it all. I just go about normal life and eventually they give up. Most of them. I have more important things to worry about.

It's time to come clean with what I know.

Julian opens the door and the sight of this man, barefoot and wearing jeans that hug his shirtless, tanned body makes me stare stupidly. The sudden presentation of all that is perfect renders me temporarily speechless, but I focus and take a deep breath, determined to not let this get too personal. I mean we've struck up a friendship. There are no ties. He doesn't owe me anything. But to say not hearing anything from him lately hasn't hurt my feelings would be lying.

"Hey," he studies me. "I was going to come and see you." He steps back and opens his door more.

"Hey," I say back as I step into his studio. "Guess I beat you to it. I noticed your lights on.

"What's up?"

"Can we sit?" I'm nervous because I don't know how all of this will end up. I don't know how I'll feel if he doesn't care that I might go home.

He indicates the chair with his arm then excuses himself and heads towards his bedroom. When he emerges, he's wearing a white shirt with the sleeves casually rolled up his forearms.

He crosses the room and sits down across from me. "The bakery will probably close for good."

He stares. Shock in his golden brown eyes. "What? How?"

"Uncle Carlos is selling. He's my sponsor. I have no clue where I stand with my permanency. So, I want to check where I stand with our contract if I do go back to Argentina."

"We can be flexible. We can call it off and just get money donated to your charity if you want, but I will need to check in with the Gala legals."

"Call it off? I'm not sure. Modeling may be a great chance for me. There's been some interest and offers from some top brand names. I think I could launch as an influencer and then be able to establish a lasting program in Argentina to assist kids to enjoy a society that embraces gender equality. All of that of that doesn't replace the fact I want to be an artist, first and foremost. But I want to make it on my own. For my talent." I take a deep breath and slowly exhale to relax my nerves.

His face softens and his attention drifts off for a second. "I'm hearing you. That's how I got here."

Okay, here goes nothing." I know who you are." I blurt out.

His attention is back to me now. "What?"

"You're Julian Blackwood, aren't you?"

He gets up fast. "No. What are you talking about? Of course I'm not."

"I prefer to be defined by my talent, not my name. I read it in an article. You said that to me."

"Coincidence."

I shake my head. "No. I know it's you and I don't get why it matters. I'm not going to tell anyone."

Julian sits again. "Dammit. I guess it had to happen sooner or later. I mean I was going to tell you when the portraits were done."

"Portraits?"

"Yeah. An abstract to sell and a Julian Blackwood portrait."

"Why not just do the abstract?"

"Because, for the first time in a very long time, I had the urge to do another portrait. Of you. But that's for my private collection."

"I'm not even going to try and understand why it's me that has that effect on you. But I'd have sat for you anytime. You only had to ask. I'm a big fan of your portrait work. Your style inspired me to embrace my own." I tell him the truth.

"Now you know who I am and it's no big deal to you, all this hiding feels a bit ridiculous. But the media attention drove me to the edge and I guess you know all about my personal life now." He half smiles, half grimaces and the pain in his eyes makes me grab his hand.

"I don't care what the headlines say. You can trust me. I never let my friends down." It's really sad that he hasn't had a friend in life to have his back.

"Not something I'm used to."

"Well, get used to it because my friendship isn't going anywhere. Be honest with me. I won't betray your trust or lose trust in you unless you prove me wrong, I expect the same from you. Friends stick by each other."

"What about more than friends?"

"Like friends with benefits?"

"Maybe. Maybe more." He shrugs but I can see in his eyes that he's sincere.

But that doesn't change the fact that he's a grown man hiding from reality and getting serious within that situation isn't my jam. Anyway, it's just too soon to make a decision about getting serious.

"Julian," I say. "How you live your life is none of my business. We have a contract, and rest assured, I will honor that. Somehow we managed to form a friendship and frankly, I don't mind making midnight booty calls. I'm an adult and I can please myself in what I do or don't do. I don't have to hide my relationships. I'm just going to ignore the media hype and get on with my life. I believe that what I do in my private life is private. That means I'm not going to go around flaunting my personal business, but I'm also not going to hide from the media either."

He nods. "You're right. I need to get on with my life and be who I am, and to hell with what's posted about me online. I know who I am and what I want."

"That is the only way I would ever consider a committed relationship with you. Otherwise, I guess we are friends, and that's always enough for me." So, the ball is in his court. With my life changing by the second, I can't commit to much else right now.

"Friends it is. Maybe some benefits." He flashes me a cheeky grin. "I'll let you take the lead there. No one has made me feel, I guess, happy... for a long time. You're more than a friend, Sofia. I hope one day soon I can prove to you that we can be together as more than friends."

"It has to happen naturally. Don't change anything for me. Do it for you and time will tell. I want to be successful under my own steam. I don't want any future success of my artwork to be because I know you. They will all say..." I don't want to sound like I'm being petty.

"Hey, you're preaching to the choir here. Do you think anyone ever thought my portraits sold because of talent and not my family name? This is the problem I have. Even now they sell and I can never be sure why. The abstracts—no one knows it's me—so any sale feels like a win." He looks down at the table.

"Your portraits sold because you are so talented. No one else paints like that. Your work might not be to everyone's taste and there will always be a contingent that just buys stuff because it's connected to someone famous, but you can't control that. There is also a huge amount of people, like me, who love what you do and buy it," I laugh a little, "as if I could even afford it. But I mean you shouldn't stop doing what you do because many people love your work. Just own it. Paint your heart and soul out and put it out there. What will be will be. But stifling all of this is not healthy, or even sane." I grin so he doesn't think I'm lecturing him too much.

"You're right. I need to get out of my head. Who cares why anyone buys it?"

"I'm not saying that. It's important to know that your work is touching people the way you want it to. It's incredibly personal to put so much of yourself on that canvas and then doubt how good it is. Maybe it's more about expressing your feelings like that than it is about what the buyers truly believe."

He nods. "Maybe."

"If you feel like I'm the muse that gets you back into doing what you love. If I can be the safe space for you to begin to express the pain inside you and find some joy again, I'd love to do that, but... I want to see the process and for you to mentor me."

"Naked?" he asks.

"Yes."

"Okay. We can do a session right now. Come and see what I've already done from memory. It needs more layers but I can take you through the process so far and you can give me your honest opinion."

"Seriously? You'd take my advice?"

"Sure. You have a good eye and all input is valuable." He leads me to the easel in his bedroom. "I dry and do touch ups in here. Work in progress but it's not hard to paint you when I can never get you out of my mind."

I suck in a breath when I see myself as he's painted me. Even unfinished, the woman looking back at me is exquisite. "Julian, that is... I mean she's stunning. That isn't me. It's not."

He turns to me. "*This* is what everyone else sees. It's the truth of who you are to the world. I can't paint subjects any other way. You are all of this and so much more I'm still trying to capture. I wish we could be more than friends, but right now, this is how I possess you."

"Maybe we are more than friends, Julian. But I don't ever want to stop being your friend. Nothing can interfere with that."

He pulls me into his arms and I feel like it's home. Like I don't need anything else in this world ever. "I don't know what we are, Sofia. But I do know, when I'm painting you, I feel alive again."

I can't help myself but kiss him in the moment of raw honesty. I feel like I have the real man here with me now and something about that touches me deep inside. I want him right now. I don't care about a lifetime. I just want to be with him in this moment and show him he can be loved for the man he is, even if we only have this one night.

"Let's go to bed." I whisper when the kiss ends.

"Are you sure?"

"I know we said one night last time. But, why not one more night? I think our friendship can handle it. Who knows what the future brings. Let's enjoy the moment."

I lie on his bed watching him take off his clothes and he's already hard. His body is so cut and perfect, I lick my lips and lock eyes with him.

"Let's take our time," he says with a sexy smile. I wish he'd smile all the time. His golden eyes could light up the room. They definitely light up my sex drive. "No hurry."

He kneels beside the bed and his hands burn into my upper thighs. I'm not sure what he's thinking. He puts light pressure on my thighs. "Let me see you."

Okay. I wasn't expecting this. I'm not sure what to do faced with him looking at my most intimate parts. My face is growing hot and my legs are not moving apart.

Julian stops at the resistance and eyes me carefully. "Sofia, is this still okay? We can stop."

Oh, way to go to show inexperience. Well done. "I don't want to stop, it's just, I didn't expect you to say that."

"You don't want me to look at you this way?"

The thought of him seeing me that way has my blood pumping like crazy and I have to admit, I'm aching for him right now. "I'm not sure. I just never... I mean no one— "

"Shit. I see. I'm sorry. I should never have presumed. You seemed so confident in what you wanted I just thought... never mind. So, no one has ever admired you like that?"

I shake my head and feel like the most naïve person in the universe.

"That's fine. It's actually amazing. I'd like to be the first, if you'll let me."

His eyes burn with desire and I swallow my reservations and relax my legs with a sigh.

"You're sure?"

"I'm sure." He's going to see me throbbing for him.

He pushes my legs open and I let it happen. I have nothing to be embarrassed about. But he goes even further and cups my ass cheeks in his strong hands and pulls me to the edge of the bed and parts me with his thumbs.

The sensation is electric.

"Sofia, your pussy is amazing. So beautiful. I want to taste you," he practically groans. He suddenly makes eye contact again. "Has anyone done that to you? With their mouth?"

I'm aching so hard at the thought. I mean I'd masturbated, I'd had orgasms, but before Julian, I'd never been penetrated before. I'd also never had anyone's mouth down there, but I'd heard it was amazing.

I shake my head. Then it's like a light goes off in his head, he looks at me even more directly. "Sofia, when we had sex, was that your first time?" He moves his hands away and helps me to sit up. He's still kneeling on the floor between my thighs.

"Yes. But it's not big deal."

"It's the biggest deal. I was so, I mean, it wasn't gentle or slow, not how a first time should be. I'm so sorry, I didn't know."

I cup Jack's face with my hand. "It was exactly how I wanted my first time to be. That's why I didn't say anything." I tell him and I mean it. "I just wanted to feel what raw, real sex was like. Not feel awkward or have you hold back."

"I definitely didn't hold back."

"It was perfect for me. I'm sorry I'm not as experienced and I've made you feel bad."

He touches my face and kisses me gently. "I don't feel bad. I feel privileged. Now, I'm going to show you how your first time should have been."

He kisses me deep and long and I melt into him. I'm surrendering to him completely. He parts my thighs again, no resistance this time. He spreads me even wider with his thumbs again. I feel his warm breath on my fully exposed clit. He blows a stream of air onto my most sensitive place and a moan escapes my lips.

God that's amazing.

"You're beautiful Sofia. Your clit is perfect. You're so wet for me. I must taste you. Would you like me to taste you?"

"Yes. Oh yes. Please. Show me how it feels." I groan, already beside myself with need. I'm aching and throbbing down there and then I feel his hot tongue sink inside me. I cry out at the shock and amazing sensation.

He doesn't stop. Just keeps sinking his tongue inside me and moving it around groaning. Then he changes and the tip of his tongue flicks softly over my clit and I shudder uncontrollably. Holy hell, this is so good. I'm not sure how much of that I can take. His flickering gets faster and harder and I'm feeling like I'm going to smash into an orgasm just when he stops and licks at my soaked opening again.

"Sofia, you taste so sweet." He mumbles before he sinks his mouth over my opening and gently sucks.

My hands are gripping the bedspread as I try to maintain control. I begin to arch up, wanting something inside me, wanting anything he has to give me. I cry out for more. I hear him chuckle and he takes his mouth off me and slides two fingers inside me. His fingertips putting pressure on the top side of my vagina.

"You're so tight. You're so good and tight. Sofia, this is your G-spot. You feel that?"

I do. I feel like I am going to turn inside out if he doesn't let me come. "Yes. God, yes. Please, I want to come."

"Not yet, baby. A little longer. Part yourself for me. Open your clit with your fingers." His voice is hypnotizing and I do as he asks. I part myself wide for him as he fills me with more fingers and assaults my clit with the flat of his tongue.

"Holy shit. Oh fuck, Oh shit. That is so good. Don't stop." My hips are in the air, grinding up to him, wanting his tongue on me harder as he massages inside me.

Then he stops licking and gently sucks my clit while flickering the very tip of his hardened tongue over my clit. I can't take anymore. I just can't.

I scream his name as my body shakes violently with the crashing orgasm, but he doesn't lick or suck harder, he slows his tongue, softens it and barely touches me with it. But each time he does my body vibrates. I'm so sensitive down there right now I push him away and he gives that deep chuckle again.

He doesn't stop. Not completely. His fingers are no longer inside me but he's still gently and softly licking at my clit. Licking up my juices and then licking back at my clit. I'm subsiding from the intensity, and I let out a deep breath.

"Wow, that was amazing."

"Are you ready?" He practically breathes the words.

'For what?"

"To come again, babe." And he goes back to work with his tongue on my clit, soft but insistent and incredibly, I feel my desire begin to rise again.

"No, no, this isn't possible, not so soon." I groan but the second orgasm is building inevitably and I'm powerless to stop it even if I wanted to. I grip the blanket again and that's not enough so I pull my legs up and back, holding them with my hands, giving him full access again.

"Perfect, Sofia. Perfect." His tongue movements get harder and faster, and I'm building in need. He parts me even wider with both hands and assaults me with the flat of his tongue again, not letting up this time. My body breaks a second time and I make noises I've never heard before and curse in Spanish.

I am only vaguely aware that Jack's body is moving, his hand pumping frantically below his waist. Then I am not the only one shuddering and uttering curses.

Somehow, Jack has achieved release too.

As I recede for the second time, he looks up and wipes his mouth. "Damn woman, you made me come then and I wasn't even inside you."

"Is that good?" I ask.

He climbs on the bed and cradles me in his arms. "That is amazing and a first for me."

Delighted, I laugh. "That's good, I have the early shift, so I best be going," I tease, and make like I'm about to leave the bed.

Jack snickers and pulls me tenderly close. "You aren't going anywhere just yet."

13

Chapter Thirteen

JULIAN

One Month Later

I open my cottage door to see Miriam do a double take and her mouth drops open for a second when she sees me.

"Welcome back, Julian." Miriam waves her hand vaguely over my body. "I need to find the amazing Sofia and thank her."

I rub my hand over my freshly shaven chin. "Damn, it's freezing without the hair. But don't just stand there." I usher her in the door. "I have something to show you."

Walking into my bedroom as Miriam follows, I use my arm to gesture the half a dozen small portraits I've completed from photos of local folks.

Miriam claps her hands in delight. "There is a God! At last. Are these for sale?"

I nod. "Soon. But the money will go back into the community somehow. I'm working on that. How's everything going that I asked you to work on?"

"The green card was sent out. Amazing how a former client in the right department can cut through red tape."

"Can't be traced back to me, though?"

"Of course not."

"The bakery?"

"Congratulations. I, for one, can't wait to see you icing cupcakes for a living."

"All staff remain there and get a raise."

"You'll need to replace Sofia. Hasn't she gone home?"

I nod. "Now she has her green card she can travel out of the country. She's picked up some major modeling contracts, so she's travelling around a bit and setting up her assistance and support centers for the youth in Argentina."

"Have a hand in all that as well, did you?"

"No. I promised her, as a friend, that I wouldn't interfere with her being successful in her own right."

"So she knows about the green card and you owning the cottages and buying the bakery now?"

"No. But that's different. She doesn't live in the cottage anymore. She should have had that green card sent out a long time ago. It was already approved. Me buying the bakery doesn't affect her work because she was going to leave anyway."

"You put the bakery in her name."

"Again, she would have managed to keep running it somehow."

Miriam shakes her head but just gets on with the next subject. "The cottage renovations are due to start next week. The architect will be here to discuss your idea of doubling the size of yours. That will probably cost a fortune with how old that place is."

"Worth it. I like it here. I'd like to make it my permanent home. The view of the mountains, the feeling I get being here. I'm sure I can make it into an amazing home."

"I guess if you throw enough money and time at something, then anything is possible. Where are you going to live in the meantime?"

We walk back out to my living area which is almost devoid of everything. "Packing is all done and I'm going to Blackwood Estate tomorrow."

"Living with your parents!? Who the hell is this person?"

I grin at her. "Would you believe me if I told you I'm going back to being an attorney?"

Miriam's broad laughter fills the almost empty space. "I am definitely not buying that."

I laugh. "You know me far too well."

"Better than you know yourself. You know cameras will be all over this."

"I don't care. I'm going on the advice of a good friend and developing a care factor of zero about what others think about me. It's what I know about myself that matters."

"I don't remember saying those *exact* words..."

I raise my eyebrows and roll my eyes, "I'm talking about Sofia. You know that."

"Replaced already."

"No one can ever replace you, Miriam."

"Bet your ass they can't. I hope all this doesn't come back to bite you."

I shrug. I hope so, too. I don't want to think about the man I was and will be again if this relationship crashes and burns over some betrayal.

"I'm flying to Buenos Aires next week for the first time. Sofia and I will be catching up." This trip to see Sofia is something I'm looking forward to immensely.

"In public?"

"Sure. I don't have anything to hide. Sofia doesn't care about click-bait headlines."

"I'm not sure she realizes quite what it's like. She's had some attention from the gala auction but being connected to you will be next level. Are you sure you can handle it?"

I nod. "Yes." The alternative is unacceptable.

Miriam is scrutinizing me with a discerning look. Finally, she nods at me. "Good luck with that."

***

Buenos Aires

One Week Later

I hop out of the car a block away from Sofia's address, my heart picking up pace as I close in on surprising her by being here. This suburb of Buenos Aires feels a world away from the manicured feel of D.C. Here, the homes are closer, with exteriors painted in vibrant colors. The community vibe is strong even from the sidewalk. Kids are running up and down the quiet street playing ball. I see folks on their front porches watching the world go by.

I'm buzzing with a mix of nerves and excitement to see her again—after all, Sofia and I have been talking every day, growing closer over calls and texts. We are friends and I like how that makes me feel. Now, I'm about to step into her world for real.

Her family home stands out as I approach. It's got that lived-in, loved-on look. The walls are painted a warm cream, looking cleaner and more cared for than some of the neighbors' places. Little details catch my eye, like the elegant shutters and a wrought-iron balcony that wouldn't look out of place in a fancier part of town. Certainly a cut above other houses I've passed so far.

As I get closer, the garden pulls me in. It's compact but lush, packed with flowers and herbs. My mom has a thing for gardening—says it keeps her grounded—so I know enough to appreciate the effort, here. The garden's not just for show; it's practical, full of plants you can actually use.

I can almost picture Sofia's mom out here, planting and pruning, making a personal mark on their spot just like my mom and me when I was small. She'd wanted to transform a huge, new-build mansion—a very impersonal building when we first moved in—into a cozy home to raise a family. I was five and remember her saying it's so big and static, she needed to make it a family home somehow and a little plot of herbs and flowers was how she started to make that happen.

The touches of extra care on Sofia's family house and the garden make it clear: this is a home of pride and aspiration, kind of like Sofia herself. She's told me about her ambitions, her drive to stand out without forgetting where she came from, and seeing her place now, it all clicks. This is where Sofia grew up, on this street, in this neighborhood. No wonder she has the soul of an artist.

I walk up to the front door, feeling like I'm crossing an important threshold. This isn't just a casual visit; it feels like I'm stepping into the heart of what's made Sofia the incredible person she is.

I knock, ready to see her and maybe learn even more about her. The house, with its personal touches and clear sense of pride, has already given me a deeper glimpse into Sofia's world—one I'm eager to become a part of, even if only for a little while.

I hear music playing and laughter coming from inside. I knock. When the door opens, I'm looking into a face that has Sofia's eyes encased in soft wrinkles and hair that's flecked with gray. I know instantly that this is her mother. The resemblance is obvious. My heart skips a beat as I imagine how Sofia will look in time. I like that thought. I want to be around to see it happen.

"Mrs. Fernandez? I'm Julian. Julian Blackwood. I wonder if Sofia might be around?"

Knowing eyes look me up and down and fix my gaze again. "Mr Blackwood. My husband and I have heard a lot about you."

"Please, call me Julian. I hope this isn't a bad time. I should've let Sofia know but I hoped to surprise her."

"Come in, Julian. I'll make tea. Sofia's father is working but Sofia is due home any moment from her lunch engagement."

Lunch engagement? Is that code for date? I mean, we're friends. Sometimes with benefits, but that doesn't mean she, we, can't date others. She has every right to make connections, to be happy. I have no right to feel jealousy but I most certainly am feeling jealous.

"It's a business lunch. You can stop worrying." Mrs. Fernandez says with humor in her eyes and a soft smile.

I let out the breath I haven't realized I'm holding and nod. "I wasn't worrying," I lie. "We're good friends, nothing more. Sofia is free to date if she chooses." I add a smile for conviction.

"If you say so. Take a seat, Julian."

I don't take a seat because my stomach is doing flips thinking about seeing her after a month and after remembering our last *friends with benefits* night together. She's so perfect for me in every way. I want to talk to her about being more than friends.

Instead, I take a moment to look around Sofia's family home. It's neat, colorful and warm-feeling.

The door bursts open and the vision that is Sofia Fernandez appears. "*Ama*! I've secured the lease for the building that will become the very first learning and support hub." In her flurry of movement and excitement, her dark gaze cased in long, thick lashes lands on me. Her eyes go wide and in the next second she's launched herself at me.

"Julian! You sly dog. You never said you were visiting. Oh. My. Goodness." She cups my smooth face and rubs my cheeks in her hands. "You look so handsome with no beard and your hair trimmed." Then she wraps her arms around me again. Her hug is like iced water to the thirsty and I'm damn thirsty, for her.

She squeezes me so tight I can't get my breath. I spin her around. "So good to see you too, Sofia. I wanted to surprise you."

"You have certainly done that." She lets me go and smiles her wide, infectious smile. "Does this mean you're back in the land of the living? Portraits and all?"

I nod. "I'm trying a new outlook on life. Something a good friend told me. Tell the world to go eff itself!" I grin.

Her mother quietly clears her throat.

"Mrs. Fernandez, forgive my manners and my language."

"Are you staying for dinner, Julian? You're more than welcome. Sofia's sisters are making empanadas and chimichurri."

I'm not sure what to say. Does Sofia's mom know about the chili incident? I don't want to sound ungracious for the offer in their family home or insult them in any way.

"*Ama* ... maybe another time. This is Julian's first time in Buenos Aires, the city that never sleeps! I think he needs to come dancing and you know I told you how he is with chili peppers."

"I'm a bit of a lightweight with spicy foods, I'm afraid, Mrs. Fernandez." I put my hands up to Sofia like a I'm warding off evil spirits. "But I'm definitely not allergic. Don't stab me again." I can't help but make fun of myself. I do see the funny side of it now. Sometimes I wonder just how I'd let myself see the world as such a dark place.

Sofia's amazing, throaty laugh fills the room and I know it's been way too long since I heard that.

When she stops her eyes twinkle at me. "I've so much to tell you. I know we communicate almost every day, but having you here is so much better. I've really missed you, Julian." Her eyes shine with sincerity and something more.

Then she's in my arms again and I hold her to me. I feel our connection and I'm hoping it's not just my wishful thinking.

"I've missed you too, Sofia. Artsbridge just isn't the same without you. None of us are."

"I'll go and make tea." Her mother disappears.

"Life has been a bit of a whirlwind lately. But I'm making progress here. I am missing the bakery and everyone. Maybe it's time I visited."

"I can fly you back anytime."

"I can get my own flight, thanks. But the bakery sold and I'm not sure I need to see that place being bulldozed down. None of the staff seem to know what's happening and they're scared. I feel responsible, somehow. Here I am enjoying my own successes but at what cost?" She looks up at me, her eyes shining with unshed tears.

Now I feel bad for keeping all this from her. "I think we both need some fun. But first, we can have dinner in my suite. I have a lot to tell you. Then, you can do the impossible and teach me to dance." I lean in and gently kiss her soft, full lips. Desire races through me. Not just sexual but the need to give her the honesty she deserves. To be the man she deserves.

Sofia sighs and holds me close again. Then she moves away and smiles. "Some fun is just what I need." Then she calls out to her mother. "No tea for us thanks, *Ama*. I'm taking Julian to see the city at night."

"Okay, Sofia. Be careful out there."

Sofia grabs my hand. "How did you get here? I'm driving *Ama's* car, but she may need it. And... you may want to rethink that suit. Change into something more casual."

"My driver is waiting around the corner. I didn't want to give away being here, so I walked a little."

"A driver and a suite? Wow, I guess life is very different for you now, or should I say, back to what passes for normal for you? Do you *want* to go into the city? I didn't even ask you. I know being in the public eye hasn't been your favorite thing to do."

"True. I'll be big news at first. Let them say what they want. If you are with me, I'll have everything I want. Eventually they'll get bored and go haunt someone else."

"And your art?"

"My art is who I am." I shrug. "I don't have to let the white noise interfere."

"Perfect. I'll grab an overnight bag." She looks at me again. "If that's okay."

"Sure. Plenty of room for a friend in my suite." I smile at her.

She's going past me towards the hallway. "What about a friend with benefits?" she whispers.

Now, a grown man has no right to be coloring up in the face, but my cheeks are burning. I'm in her parent's home and that catches me off guard. "I'll go grab the car and meet you out front." I say quickly.

"I'm grabbing a bag and leaving, Ama." Sofia calls out as I open the front door to leave. "Julian is leaving now."

"Okay, nice to meet you, Julian. Take care of my girl. I won't wait up, Sofia," she calls out like it's the most natural thing in the world. I make a hasty retreat as I say my goodbyes and shut the front door behind me.

Right now, I definitely feel like an awkward teenager. I have the raging hormones of one as well, and I may be doing more than changing my clothes back in my suite.

14

C hapter Fourteen

SOFIA

"Would you like a champagne, or maybe a cocktail? The butler service will get whatever you want." Julian says as we enter the Alvear Suite at the Park Hyatt.

My eyes can't take in enough of the features at once. "I didn't realize you meant a suite at the Hyatt. Wow, this is huge." It's amazing in here. Persian rugs and a fireplace. Not full of chandeliers and over-the-top decor but it's spacious and sumptuous. Really classy with heritage charm and character.

"I guess I did splurge a little. However, I was hoping to invite a friend over." He grins at me and how handsome he is makes me a little speechless.

I'm glad I got to know him as Jack because Julian is everything that is way too good and intimidating for me. "I'm sure you have a million friends keen to get in here with you." Insecurities flash through my mind.

"But only one I choose to be here." He takes me in his arms again. "I've never met anyone who gives me the confidence to be who I am like you do, Sofia."

"You make me feel like I can take on the world, too."

"Now, how about that drink?" Julian asks again.

"I've been off alcohol lately. Boring I know, but it just makes me feel nauseated. Iced tea would be amazing though."

"Iced tea it is. I don't think I need alcohol either. After that long flight I'd probably fall straight asleep. Not my intention tonight. I need energy for dancing." His demanding mouth is on mine again and I meet his passion.

My heart races and the ache deep inside me explodes into a torrent of desire. Our tongues meet like molten lava and I fist his short cropped hair, pulling him in harder enjoying the smoothness of his face against mine. My leg snakes around his as I press myself to his rock-hard thigh.

He moves his leg to stimulate my pussy and I groan into his mouth. The kiss breaks and he whispers my name. The need in him is evident as I lower my hand to his hardened manhood. I know what I want and he clearly wants me, too.

"Let's shower."

"Sounds perfect."

He leads me in through the bedroom and past the massive bed. A double-headed shower is waiting in an opulent ensuite bathroom. "Get undressed, Sofia."

I like the hunger in his eyes as I peel off my clothes to stand naked before him. It's not like I've never done this before but this time he's seeing me with the fire and sexual need of a man, rather than from an artist's eye. I know my face is red from his intimate scrutiny and remembering the first time he used his mouth to bring me to multiple orgasms. "Your turn."

I watch him strip off his clothing and while I've seen him naked before, this time there's an openness about it that I like. It feels more honest somehow and I like it. I like everything about Julian Blackwood, right now. He steps into the shower and waves his hand over a panel. Steamy water immediately starts from both showerheads. I take the hand he offers me and he draws me into the water beside him.

"Sofia, you're beautiful. Perfect."

"I'm not perfect. No one is. But thank you."

"You are perfect for me. Touch me, Sofia. Show me how you want me."

My hands span his broad, muscled chest, the spattering of dark blond hair soft underneath my palms. Trailing over his taut nipples, I trace ever lower to his ripped abdomen, following the outline of the perfect V and his engorged cock. He shudders under my touch and the power of this moment surges through me. I drop to my knees and study his perfect maleness, warm water cascading off him.

I have an urge to do something I've only heard and read about. Something I've fantasized about alone in my room, late at night. I gently massage underneath him and his cock jumps and twitches. There's a droplet at the tip, somehow clinging there even with the water. I softly let my tongue taste him there. The smoothness of the head of his erection thrills me and I slowly close my lips over the entire head and swirl my tongue around.

Julian groans above me, his hands cradling my head gently, guiding me, encouraging me with his soft moans. His scent, the heat of the shower steam, and the sound of the water amplifies every sensation, making this moment pulse with intensity.

I take him deeper, the throbbing pulse of him matched by my own racing heart. His hips twitch forward instinctively, and I meet him eagerly, exploring this new intimacy with curiosity and desire. I want to give him as much pleasure as he's given me, to learn what makes him lose control. I draw back and take him in again, keeping the pace even and sucking as I draw back. He grows incredibly larger under my mouth action and I struggle to take his engorged cock in completely. He's an incredible man when fully aroused.

He is panting heavily now, moaning and shaking. "That's it. Do me just like that, Baby," he cries. The cry sounds mindless with a desperate need to climax and I find it sexy as hell. His grip tightens on my hair, not painfully, but a tell that he is about to come undone. I am ready and eager to accept all of what he has to give. Suddenly, I feel him shudder and jerk and my mouth floods with the sweet essence of him.

Julian's head is back, mouth open in ecstasy, chest heaving. He pulls back slightly, lifting me to my feet. "Sofia, you are amazing," he murmurs, his voice thick with arousal. He turns me gently against the glass shower wall, my hands bracing against the glass and Julian pressed close in behind me, this positioning is new for us and my desire is electric. The contrast of the hot water and the cool glass sends shivers down my spine. Julian's hands roam over my body, tracing the water droplets down my back, over my hips and down my thighs.

His touch is both a question and an answer, seeking and finding the places he knows make me gasp, tremble, and moan. His fingers find me, slick and wanting, and he teases my most sensitive place—a place he knows well—with a touch that's both tender and insistent, driving me towards a precipice I'm all too eager to leap from. But I don't want to finish like this. I want him throbbing inside me.

"Julian, please," I breathe out, my voice barely a whisper over the sound of the shower.

He obliges, his body aligning with mine, his erection pressing insistently at my entrance. Slowly, he presses his hardness inside me, and we both catch our breath at the sensation. He doesn't hesitate any longer, his cock fills me completely and I arch back to him, inviting him deeper. Now, moving with a rhythm that is both new and as old as time, our wet, soapy bodies slide together, the heat building between us rivaling the steam that fills the room.

Then his gentleness changes to something more raw and insistent. Harder thrusts, pounding deeper inside me and I press back wanting it all. His fingernails graze my skin as he thrusts.

His mouth finds my neck, his teeth nipping my skin, not softly, and I know he's marking me in a way that feels right—like claiming and being claimed all at once. I tilt my head back, giving him better access, lost in the sensation of him moving within me, around me, as a part of me.

"Look at us," Julian whispers, his hand guiding mine to the glass shower wall, now fogged with steam. He wipes a small circle clear with his palm. Our reflection in the huge mirror is hazy but unmistakable—two figures intertwined, moving in a dance both primal and profoundly intimate.

Parts of me are pressed against the glass, and his fingers are clutching at my hips. His mouth is nipping and sucking my neck and shoulder, and his eyes are on me in the mirror. A look of pure want and need on our faces; his passion and my passion, both about to explode.

In this steamy, blurred image, I see not just Julian and me but a possibility of us that terrifies and exhilarates me in equal measure. I know we're crossing lines that won't easily be uncrossed, but in this moment, with the heat and the water and his body joined with mine, his eyes staring into mine I don't want to think about lines. I only want to feel, to be, to lose myself in the man who sees me not just as I am, but as I could be.

Our movements grow more urgent and desperate, as we chase a climax that looms just on the edge of our joined breaths. When it comes, we don't look away from each other in the reflection. We watch the crescendo of sensation that takes our faces through a myriad of expressions. He cries out my name and I shout his as the shared, shuddering orgasm leaves us clinging to each other, panting, spent, and more connected than I could have ever imagined.

As the water continues to pour over us, rinsing away any barriers I might have had left, I realize that no matter what comes next, this moment will forever define a part of who we are—together. He pulls himself away from me and I turn to face him. Both our slick bodies pressing together as I pant and try to catch my breath.

"I love you, Sofia Ferandez."

The tears fill my eyes and I've never felt anything so right in my life. "I love you too, Julian."

And I do. I really do. I want us to be able to make this work, so badly. I hope we can.

***

"Mmmmm." I nuzzle his neck and imagine waking up to this every morning. "I guess we didn't get much dancing done."

"Not exactly. But there's always tonight," he says while touching my face and kissing me. "We didn't get much talking done either, and there are a few things I'd like to tell you."

My heart races now. Is he about to give me the 'I'm sorry, but I'm not ready to do the whole public thing with you' speech or the 'it was the heat of the moment' spiel? I know we both confessed our love at the time in the shower, but does that really mean anything? We'd spent most of the night exploring each other and neither of us said it again. I'm not going to overthink it.

"I want to be honest with you. You once said the only way you would consider a relationship with me was through me being honest and being myself."

Wait. Is he saying he wants us in a committed relationship? Like living together or something? I'm not sure I'm ready for that. "Julian, I—"

"I bought the bakery," he interjects.

"What?" I push myself up on one elbow.

"Does that upset you?"

"I'm not sure how to feel really." It's true. This news has taken me by surprise. I turn it over in my mind and then settle on how I feel. "I'm relieved it's you. Unless you're going to knock it down and build a high-rise."

"I can't imagine a high-rise ever going into Artsbridge," he answers and brushes my hair off my face. "I want to keep the bakery the same as much as you do. We have some very special memories there and the rest of the crew really need the work. Plus, it gives you something to fall back on whenever you need it."

I eye him suspiciously, "What do you mean by that?" Does he mean he doesn't think I'll be successful so I'll need a backup career?

He climbs out of bed giving me the pleasure of admiring his perfectly sculpted naked body as he pads across the deep-pile carpet to his suitcase, pulling on some boxers. "I put the bakery in your name, Sofia. I think it's only right that it stays in your family."

He did *what*? I scramble out of bed now and pull on a short dress and panties. "I don't understand what you're saying. I mean I understand but why would you just do that? I made it very clear I wanted to get whatever I get on my own."

He nods. "With your art career."

"With my life." I glare at him. "You could have discussed it with me at least, made an arrangement for me to pay you back."

He flicks his hand in the air as he opens a bottled water. "There's no need. It was just something I wanted to do at the time. I felt it solved a lot of hassles and we could discuss it later. Which we are now. Shall we order breakfast? How do you like your eggs?"

"Julian, I'm not interested in damned eggs! You can't just go around gifting bakeries like boxes of chocolates."

He frowns a little. "Look, what is the actual problem here? If you don't want the bakery, resell it or something."

I'm feeling everything we just shared last night, the closeness, the hope of us being able to have a committed relationship all flying out of the window with his assumption that I'd ever be okay about this. "The fact that you even have to ask me that question shows how little you know me, even after all this time being friends. We've talked about this stuff."

He sighs and shakes his head. "I don't get it. I'm sorry I've upset you. I just made a decision at the time."

"Exactly, a decision that could change my whole life and you didn't think to ask me about it. This is why I never wanted to be involved with anyone with money like you have. I don't want your help like that. I don't need problems magically fixed for me. I want you, Julian. The man. As a friend and if it is to be anything more, I need to be in control of where my life goes. Make my own successes and failures."

His frown deepens as he comes over to take me in his arms. "I must be an idiot because I'm struggling to see the problem in either. The bakery is a business deal. I make them all the time. Real estate is how I started to make my own money and I'm always scouting for viable opportunities."

"Good for you." I shouldn't be sarcastic but his lack of understanding is infuriating. But I need to think logically about this and not let emotions drive how I feel. I'm sure he's done all of this in good faith, and not in an effort to control me. However, I need him to understand why it's important. I need to communicate it better. I take a deep breath and relax a little. I'm not into arguing.

"Are we okay?" Real concern etches his face.   Julian's gaze is intense. "There's something else you should know. I own the cottage you rented and the one I lived in."

"You what? Since when? I mean, when did you buy them?"

"Shortly before I moved in there."

I shake my head in disbelief. "So, you were my landlord and the improvements and the fixed rent payment was all you?" I consider this additional fact, turning it over in my mind. Yet one more new thing I didn't know about Julian. It isn't so much that I didn't know he owned the cottages, but more about not knowing a fact about something essential to my life, like to whom I was paying rent.

"Please tell me we are okay."

"Look, I'm not trying to be difficult or ungracious. It's not like you gave me free rent. You just fixed what really needed fixing; you didn't give the place a glam makeover.. We had no relationship then. That's the reason I'm okay with that" I explain.

He looks relieved. "I'm in the process now of having them preserved but I also have plans to enlarge mine by adding a whole new living section on to it."

"Wow, that will take a lot of work."

He shrugs, "I have time."

I'm silent while my mind continues to process everything I've learned. One thing is driving me to speak. "Just to be clear, the bakery purchase and gifting is very different in my mind. That's crossing a personal line. That is going into my life and assuming how I'll feel. I don't feel comfortable with that. You must understand, it's similar to the media reporting what you're wearing that day as opposed to making a judgment on your personal life and who you are."

He shrugs, "You're right. I can see it now. I'm sorry. I won't do that again. Just assume I know how you feel, I mean. I'll check in and ask."

"I appreciate that. Now, if the cottages are being renovated, where will you paint in the meantime? Do you have another place?"

Maybe he's moving back to D.C. and selling them.

"I'm taking a leaf out of your book and going back home for a few months. I own properties, so it's not like I need to, but I feel I need to connect back to my roots, and my father and I have a lot of years to make up. We spent most of those years at loggerheads. I understand why he pushed for me to follow in his footsteps. It was just never going to happen. Now, I'd like to know him better as a friend." He smiles at me. "I'm finding a lot of value in friends lately."

"You can learn a lot about yourself when you understand the people your parents are." My mom will always be my best friend. And my father, well—like you I guess—I accept why he pushes me the way he does. It's never going to be the way he wants it to be, but I get why he's wired that way and I love him. He's provided a stable home for us and that's more than a lot of kids get. I'd just love him to be proud of my achievements someday." I get closer to Julian and he encircles me with his arms. It still hurts that my father can't see me for who I am, a strong, independent, successful woman, and be proud. One day I swear I will make him proud of me for all the right reasons.

Julian holds me for a while longer before he speaks again. "In the spirit of me being open and honest. I want us to be more than friends, and more than friends with benefits. I want you in my life. I think I've made that clear. How do you feel about that?"

"I'm not sure." I don't want to give my heart and be hurt, but my career is also going to take me away a lot. I need to focus on my art. Is the timing right?

Julian kisses me softly. "Sofia, I need you in my life. You make me a better man."

"I'm glad you feel that way, but I'm not looking to save anyone or be anyone's mother. What about the media attention? Is it something you can handle long term, because I also don't want to become a broody hermit artist any time in the future."

The thought of getting into something serious and then finding out Julian can't handle it is not something I can do. If he wants to go into hiding again, I can't do that with him. I can't expect him to put up with intrusions into his character by the media either, but only he can steel himself against it. Is he really ready?

"I don't care about what the media cooks up. I really don't. You are what's important. *We* are." Sincerity shines from his golden eyes. "I can do this with you by my side, Sofia."

How do I ever say no to this man and break his heart? So, I need to be sure he gets where I'm coming from and why.

"What's more important is, can you do it without me by your side. Are you ready? If you are ready to be honest with us being in a relationship and do the work to have me in your life, it could work. You know I feel more for you than just friendship. I said so in the shower, but it's very important to me that you aren't just throwing money at things to fix them for me and that you'll stand by me in whatever decisions I make. And that you are in a solid place with the media with or without me."

"I understand. It's about integrity."

"Not just that, Julian. All my life I've heard from my father that boys are more important than girls. More valuable because they are the breadwinners, the head of the household, the reason why women are able to live and breathe. I've heard how disappointed he was to get four daughters, especially with the eldest—me—not being male."

I swallow my pain and keep my voice steady because I need to get the man I love to understand how deeply this affects my life.

"That's a very old-school attitude."

"Not in all cultures. I love my father. He is a good man. He's a hard worker and I know he wants the best for me. But him thinking my body is my only worthwhile commodity—to marry me into money and save myself—well, that cuts deep.

I will prove these attitudes are harmful and outdated, and I will give today's youth everything I can to see changes. But will I ever hear him say he's proud of me for anything like that? Probably not." I pause and get back to my point. "To teach girls that their education is every bit as important as boys. To help boys see that girls are their equal as humans even if there are differences in what they do best. Everyone brings something to the table."

"I'm positive you will make a difference." Julian smiles and nods. "I've never known anyone more sure of themselves."

"But that's just it, Julian. I'm not so sure of myself inside. If I'm with you, my father will think I'm doing exactly what I've always argued with him about. Your family may think I'm using you to get where I want to be in life. I don't want that. When your every achievement is ridiculed and told it's a waste of time—worth nothing—something inside you begins to believe that's true."

"It's not true and you know it isn't. But doesn't this fall into the same category as me worrying too much about why my portraits are selling? Does it matter what they all think if you know in your heart that you have worked and earned everything yourself?"

He's right, I know he is. "I'm not saying you're wrong about that. But I'm also not ready to have my father say he's right. I need to set a strong example to my sisters. If we are to be together, in a committed relationship, you must let me have my own successes even if it means failure. And you must unapologetically be with me because of who I am, not because of how I look. No running and hiding. I'm not saying to kiss and tell nor tell our life story, but before you say anything, or buy anything, or make a decision that can change my life, please discuss this with me first. Above all Julian, take care of my heart."

Julian pulls me in close, almost squeezing the air out of me. "I promise, Sofia. Your heart is safe with me."

15

C hapter Fifteen

JULIAN

I'd stayed the whole week in Buenos Aires and I'm exhausted yet completely refreshed all at the same time. It really is the city that never sleeps, and we hadn't had a whole lot of sleep for reasons other than dancing. I wish I could keep my hands off her but it's impossible. Luckily, she feels the same. "When do you need to be in Los Angeles?" I ask her.

"The end of next week. I must book my tickets. I'm excited for my first red-carpet event with Rialto Jewelry. We launch the first of a series of adverts. I'm super nervous."

"Do you have a date? I mean have they requested you attend with someone they've arranged?"

Sofia looks at me with wide eyes. "Do they do that?"

"Sometimes, and they should have arranged security for you." My mind is going over all the things Sofia won't possibly know about the world she's about to enter. A world I know all too well.

"Security? Why on earth would I need that?"

"Because you'll be dripping in their most expensive diamonds."

"Surely they have good fakes they use for such things."

"That is not their style. Would you consider me flying us over in my private jet and me attending with you?" I'm trying not to sound like I'm being controlling or assuming.

"Is this your launch back into the world?"

"Probably, but it's not about that. I can organize security. I have the best. I'd like to support you in your first real time in the public eye. It can be a lot."

Sofia nods. "I think I'd like that. But the private jet seems a bit much. I'm happy to fly economy."

"I think you'll find that isn't Rialto Jewelry's style either. I know you won't want to cut into the money you have flying first class and I have business in Los Angeles. It's a win-win."

She considers this. "If you have to be there anyway, I guess I can hitch a ride. Thank you for asking and not assuming you know what's best for me. You're flying out of here today, though. Doesn't that mean you have to come all the way back to get me?"

"Not if you come too."

"Me? Today? I'm not sure."

"Only if you don't have anything important to do here for a couple of weeks, and there is the bakery to discuss. I can resell it if you don't want it. For now, it's running as normal but none of the staff know who's bought it."

She considers what I've said for a few minutes. "Will you allow me to pay you back for the bakery? I'd need to see exactly what you paid for it and pay interest."

"I can have a contract drawn up."

"A normal, everyday, business loan contract."

"No problem."

"In that case, I guess I own a bakery. I've missed the crew so much and I'm long overdue to catch up with Bailey. She's thinks her relationship with her fiancé may be coming to an end, and she's been a bit down because of all the years they both put into that relationship."

"I'm sorry to hear that. Break-ups can be hard, but maybe this is just a rough patch they can get over."

I sigh. "Rob is a great guy, but it seems to me that they make better friends than a romantic couple, but what do I know? I'm not exactly brimming with experience to be making that kind of judgement call for someone else. All I know is that my cousin deserves all the passion and love this world has to offer."

Sofia's eyes take on a certain glow when she's talking about the people she loves most in the world. I hope she looks like that when she's talking about me. "I'm sure she'll find her happiness."

"Just like me. Do you have any single brothers?" Sofia laughs.

"Actually, I do have one. But he's not into settling down, so steer clear of that."

I think of Darien and his eternal bachelor wish. At least I'd tried to love and settle down in my younger days. He acts like he's allergic to the very thought. Maybe he needs someone to smash him with an EpiPen to get him to change his mind. I realize my attention has drifted and I focus back on Sofia's words.

"I want to talk to you about how I go about setting Bailey up as my manager. She's so switched on when it comes to making deals and no one has my best interests at heart like she does. For now, I'm hoping she takes on the running of the bakery until we find the right person, but after that, I'd like her to work closely with me."

"I'll talk to Miriam. She can advise you both on that and let you know how to make it happen."

"Oh wait. I just realized I don't have a cottage to stay in and Bailey and Rob are still living in an efficiency apartment until after they marry and buy a house—at least that was the plan. I don't want you wasting money on accommodation for us."

Where will we stay? Will we even stay together? I can easily guess her mind is running at a million miles an hour with those questions.

"Come and stay at Blackwood Estate. There's heaps of space and my mother will be eternally grateful that I've bought a girl home, finally."

She stares at me like I've said something to knock the world off its axis. "You've never done that before?"

I shake my head. "Not to stay."

"But you were married."

"Yes," I think back on those years and how I could tell my mother was only tolerating my ex-wife. "Let's just say they didn't have enough in common with each other that I would put them in the same house together for more than a few hours."

"Oh." Sofia looks down and frowns.

"Don't worry, Mom will love you."

"But what if she doesn't?"

"If she doesn't then we'll stay elsewhere, but you have nothing to worry about."

"And your father? I know you haven't had the best history with him."

"Look, we are all adults and you are my choice. You have nothing to worry about. I know they will love you and I've got you."

Her wide smile has returned, and she flicks her hair back. No wonder the most prestigious jewelry company in the world has secured her for their advertisements. She's such a natural beauty. "Okay. Let's give it a shot. But I may need a night or two to catch up with friends and go out clubbing or something."

"Clubbing in Artsbridge?" I laugh. "Good luck with that."

She playfully slaps my arm. "We'll go to the city. I'll book us a house or something."

"You are free to come and go as you please. And you have your freedom. I don't need to be with you twenty-four-seven."

"It's not that I don't want you to join us..."

"I know. But you need to be able to speak your truth with them your way. I get that. You go see them and let me know when to pick you up for Blackwood Estate."

"Done deal."

***

"Julian, you've shaved and had a haircut." Mom hugs me and squeezes both my cheeks at the same time. "Thank goodness. Are you painting portraits again?"

"A few. Mom, I need to stay here while I get renovations done."

"Renovations? Where?"

"Artsbridge. I'll be living there when the work is done."

"Stay here as long as you want. Your room is still the same. Come into the kitchen, I have cookies baking."

"I'd prefer the guest wing until next week." I say as I follow her into the kitchen. The scent of fresh-baked cookies fill the air. "Then I'm in Los Angeles for a week.

"Guest wing? I guess so. We don't have any guests coming. Why don't you want your room?"

I guess I may as well tell her. "I'm bringing a guest."

Mom spins around. "Male or female?"

"Female. Her name is Sofia."

"Oh, I see. Yes, I guess you don't want her in there with your private collection." Mom nods like she and I share some secret.

"What do you know about my private collection? I hope you haven't been snooping."

"No, of course not. But it's not a secret that you have one, I just assumed you keep it in there somewhere."

True, the media has speculated over this aspect of my life for years. Someone I once called my friend spilled a lot of tea about me for a substantial amount of money in my early years of being an attorney. Mom is right. It is in there, safely packed away. The only one I really need to add is Sofia's. I have it in storage.

The other nude portraits in my private collection need to be destroyed, I'd hate any of them ever getting leaked in the news. Apart from avoiding lawsuits I'd hate for any of the women I've previously been on an intimate level with having their privacy breached in such a way. It's time I dealt with the portraits personally and see they are disposed of permanently.

"So, Julian?" Mom is grinning from ear to ear. "Are you *sharing* the guest wing with your guest?"

"Probably."

"You've never spoken of her before."

"We've been friends for a while. She has a red-carpet event in Los Angeles, so we'll fly there together."

"A red-carpet event!? You're ready to put yourself back out there? Are you sure?"

I nod. "I'm okay."

"I really hope so, son."

I give her a hug. "Don't fuss, Mom. I just needed some time out. I'm sorry my time in Artsbridge stressed you out so much."

"I'm just glad you're ready to get back into life and with a lady friend." She pats my arm. "That will do you good. I can't wait to meet this mystery woman you've had hidden away. Are you serious about her? Is there anything I should know before I meet her?"

"No pressure please. Give her chance."

"Of course. Where's she from?"

"I met her in Artsbridge, she worked in her Uncle's bakery but she was born in Argentina. Buenos Aires."

"Oh. Is she looking to move to the USA? You know some women—"

"Sofia has her green card, and she has her own career. She's fiercely independent, so don't suggest anything of the sort. If you'd like to know more about her, you can ask her yourself when she visits."

Mom smiles at me. I know she means well. My track record hasn't been great.

"You know the media won't let this go unnoticed. They will pick up on that and anything else they can hound you both with. I hope Sofia is ready for that."

"We have nothing to hide. They'll give up on us eventually."

"One can only hope." Mom's frown shows her worry.

"Julian? Well, aren't you full of surprises. Good to see you." My father's voice booms around the kitchen. "What's going on with you, apart from grooming?"

I grin at Dad as he strides up to shake my hand. I start to speak but Mom beats me to it.

"Julian has a girlfriend and he's bringing her to stay. In the guest wing. Together." Mom gushes.

"A girlfriend? Well, that's great." My father pats my shoulder, "could this be *the one*?"

"Dad, it's no big deal and I don't want a big deal made out of it. Keep it low-key." The pressure to find a woman to marry and settle down with runs strong. I know I want to be with Sofia but I don't want her to feel pressured. "It's early days."

"Her name is Sofia and he met her in a bakery. She's from Buenos Aires," Mom says.

"When were you in a bakery in Buenos Aires?" Dad asks.

I shake my head. "The bakery is in Artsbridge, Dad. Sofia was born in Buenos Aires."

"Oh. Not one of those is she?"

My patience is wearing thin on this subject.

"She has her own career and already has a green card." Mom says before I get a chance.

"Right." Dad sounds unconvinced. "The media will love this."

"Honestly, just stop. I'm not living my life worried about headlines anymore. I'll cancel the whole damn thing and stay at a hotel. I don't know why you'd worry about the media scrutinizing me when my own family is doing a great job. I thought you guys would have my back."

"We do have your back, don't we, Charles? We really do."

"Then don't say all of this crap that will highly offend a good friend of mine who will be here as a guest. I *did* want her to meet you."

"So is she a friend, or, more?" Dad looks confused.

"We've been friends. I'd like it to be more. But we all know it's not easy dating a Blackwood, especially me. Can we just meet her before we make any decisions on the type of person she is?" I'm trying to not overreact.

"I'm with you, Julian. Let's not overthink this. It'll be an honor to welcome her to our home." Dad says.

"Of course it is. I can't wait to meet her." Mom pulls the cookies out of the oven and places them on the cooling rack. "We'll have a family dinner."

"Mom, I don't think that's needed." Maybe it's way too soon for that. I'm not sure.

"Nonsense. Your father loves a chance to use the grill. If Sofia is the person you say she is, she'll fit right in with everyone."

I know this means a lot to Mom because my ex-wife only ever came to one family dinner. She said my family was too much, that they hated her. I wasn't sure back then but after the way my ex betrayed me, maybe she was just saying that because my family had her pegged from the start. Or maybe my family did go too far when I wasn't around. I always felt like I was calming the waters with either my mom or my wife.

What if they offend Sofia in the same way, somehow? This is why I prefer not to deal with feelings. But feelings are what I have with Sofia. Strong feelings and I want to protect her from that type of hurt.

16

Chapter Sixteen

SOFIA

"Get the frick out of town! Look who the cat's dragged in." Eddie rushes up to me and pulls me into a hug. "Sofia, girl, you look stunning. I've missed you so much."

"I've missed you too, Eddie. So much. Is Gus still here and Jordan?"

"Sure. We're all still on deck. It's been a busy morning. You know how some Fridays get. Not that you'd know it at the moment." He holds me at arm's length. "Let me look at you. Hmmmm. Have you been seeing a certain grumpy husband lately?"

I feel my face flush and Eddie laughs.

"I knew it!"

"I'm not here to discuss my private life."

"Oh, but you will be. We're not letting you off that easily. Does Bailey know you're here?"

"Yes, I've messaged her. She'll be here shortly."

I walk to the service counter. "Hey Ava. How're the twins?"

"Oh, Sofia. They are growing fast but school is good for them and lets me work more regular hours." She looks down, "but now the bakery's been sold I wonder if I'll even have a job."

"I'm sure everything will be fine." I say and she smiles slightly.

"I wish I could be so positive."

"Sofia! Nice to see you." Gus comes over. "How's life?"

"Great thanks, Gus. How about you?" I say and watch him wondering whether to hug me or not. He's not a hugger. I reach my arms out and draw him in. "Come here, you big lug. I've missed you." I give him a tight squeeze and his low laugh rumbles.

"Welcome back," he says as he moves away. "Jordan," he calls out the back. "Sofia is here."

I hear some curse words before Jordan comes running from out back and fist bumps me. "Good to see ya."

I hear the door behind me and Bailey hugs me from behind. "Oh my God, the gang's all back together. Never leave me for that long again."

I grip her arms. Boy, have I missed my best friend in the world. "I promise I won't."

She lets me go and I'm ready to tell them all my news. "Can you give me some time to chat to you all? A lot has happened."

"She means grumpy husband," Eddie says fanning his face. "They've been hot and heavy."

"This has nothing to do with Julian." I keep my cool and smile.

"I still can't believe the most unkempt, moody man turned out to be a super-rich guy. It's like a real-life fairy tale." Eddie says and the rest of them nod.

I look at Bailey and raise my eyebrows. She shakes her head.

"How do you know about that?" I quiz Eddie. I hadn't told anyone else but Bailey.

"Oh, honey. It's all over the socials this past twenty-four hours. Have you been under a rock?" Ava adds.

I had been distracted and I'd slept on the private jet for almost all of the trip and then I'd come straight here. "I haven't looked at my phone or socials since I landed. The battery needs charging. I guess it doesn't matter anyway. I mean, we're bound to get attention."

"Yes, it's not every day a billionaire gets you a green card. Go you!" Jordan says and Eddie smacks her on the arm. "What!?" She glares at him. "I'm just joking."

"Not funny, Jord. You know how Sofia feels about that stuff."

My heart pounds and I feel nausea in the pit of my stomach. "Someone better show me what this is all about." But I also know I can't let this overshadow the reason I've come to see everyone today.

I take a deep breath. Julian did warn me that the media would do this. I assured him I'd be okay with it. But that can come later. I need to tell the best crew in the world something exciting and the bullshit the media cooks up can wait. I got this.

"Stop keeping us in suspense, then. I have dough waiting," Gus urges.

"I bought the bakery."

"Wow! I mean, you did? That's great." Bailey is talking and looking at me like 'why didn't I know about this already?'

I nod. "It's been a sudden development."

"How so?" Eddie asks.

"Can we go and sit down?" I walk towards one of the larger tables and sit. My head is a little spinny right now. Must be all the excitement.

They all sit.

"Alright. I'm buying the bakery from the person who bought it. What I'm here to find out is, are you all staying on and would you all be interested in owning it together? Like a percentage to each of you?"

They are all staring at me like I've just told them aliens have landed.

"I know, it's a lot. While I'd love to be able to come back and run the bakery, that won't be able to happen for a while. I know you all like family. I trust you all. Take some time to think about it."

I turn to Bailey. "I know things may be changing in your life and you're at a crossroads, but I'd love you to be the manager here. If that's something that fits into your world right now."

"I'm in. Yes." Bailey doesn't hesitate to have my back.

"Only if it's what you really want. What you all want." My gaze encompasses them all.

They all nod but still look blindsided.

"After Los Angeles, I'll come back and we'll go through it all in more detail. Wait till then to make a solid decision if you need the time to think or talk it over with anyone. If you need legal advice, Miriam is setting aside some time. Bring any possible issues to me and we'll try and work it out."

"This is an awfully big gesture, Sofia." Gus says. "Are you sure?"

I smile, feeling relieved. "Never been more sure of anything. Gus, what I've gotten here is everything—the support, the love, the friendship. You're the hardest workers I know. I'm absolutely certain."

The first of the lunchtime guests start trickling in and the team bounds into action.

"I'll see you all soon. I'll message you and we'll get together on a Sunday." They all hug me in turn, except Gus and Jordan. But I get a fist-bump from Jordan and notice unshed tears glittering in her eyes. I never realized this offer would touch them so deeply.

"We need to go somewhere and talk. I got you, but how on earth did this happen?" Bailey asked. "Last I heard you'd depleted your money securing a lease and equipment for the first learning and support center. And this online crap. I mean, I'm not sure you're ready."

"I'm okay. I said I would be and I will be."

"Maybe you just shouldn't read it then. You've never been a gossip column reader anyway. No need to start now."

I know she's right. But after I found out he'd bought the bakery and put it in my name, and then learned that he owned the cottage where I not only lived, but whose ancient appliances were all upgraded after we became friends, something inside me wants to know what they are saying about the green card situation. "I can't hide from it forever. Besides there's a lot more we need to discuss. How about a boozy lunch?"

"You are speaking my language. Come and see my new place. I have tacos and wine."

"Perfect."

Bailey and I always pick up right where we leave off no matter how long it's been since we've seen each other. Having a cousin like her is amazing. Not only does she get me as a person, but she understands the cultural pressures and why I'm so driven to be successful and make positive changes to future generations. She really sees me.

I'm hoping one day, Julian will be able to see me like that and understand it. I guess that's what going to his family home is all about for me. It's scary, but I have to know his family could take me in as one of them before I fully commit to Julian.

***

"Wait. Am I hearing you right? Julian bought the bakery and gave it to you?" Baileys eyes are wide and she sips her wine.

I nod. "He tried, yes. But once I found out, I told him that I would only accept it as a business loan with interest."

"Do you think the bakery income can support all of us and make the payments?"

"I do. Especially with Tio Carlos not spending money like he was. But we also need to be a real team and grow the business. That's why I need you to head up the crew. I also want some more staff so we can open Sundays. But they need to fit our vibe, you know?"

"This breakup has made me realize there's a whole world out there to explore," Bailey starts.

My heart is in my throat. Breakup? Maybe she's moving on from Rob and her plans for a life with him. I have to support her if she is.

"I want to get a business degree and then leadership and management. This is perfect for me."

My heart swells and my eyes prickle with tears. "Thank the gods for that. I'm not sure I could do this without you."

"Are you on your period? You look like you're tearing up. It's not that big of a deal."

"I'm regular so far." Although my last one was erratic and more spotting than flow. But that happens sometimes. "The pill keeps it that way, that's why I like being on it."

"And the fact that you can have impulsive sex if the chance arises, so to speak." She grins. "Which is has and more than once. Are you and Julian okay? I mean hot sex is one thing but I know you're struggling with it being friends or more. How are you coping with all of that?"

She's right. My emotions are all over the place lately. I take a sip of red wine but the second it hits my nostrils and touches my lip, my stomach turns over violently. I rush to the kitchen sink and try to vomit. Nothing comes up but I'm hot and sweaty and I heave.

"Fuck! Sofia, are you okay? Maybe you got a virus on the plane."

I splash my face with water and Bailey hands me a clean towel. "I'm okay. I just forgot alcohol isn't agreeing with me right now."

"Oh you poor bitch." Bailey laughs. "That would be the worst thing in the world to happen."

"I think maybe I've been overdoing things." I go and sit back down as Bailey washes the wine down the sink.

She puts a glass of iced water in front of me. "Here, just in case you have picked up a virus. Economy can be dicey."

"Except I flew in Julian's private jet."

"You did what now?"

I smile. "He was coming back and he has an art show in Los Angeles, so I am staying with him at his family home and we are going to the Rialto Jewelry event as a couple."

Bailey swallows all of her wine in one gulp. "Wait. Let me get this straight. You're flying around in a private jet, going to your first red-carpet event as a couple, and you are going to meet the family?" She grabs my left hand and stares at my bare finger. "Why the hell isn't there a diamond on here?"

"I'm not sure I want that. You know how important it is to me to make my own success. I'm not sure his family and I will be a good fit. There's only one way to find out, right?"

"For someone who loves a simple life, you sure have complicated the shit out of yours. Have you, and him... well, you know," She waggles her eyebrows, "said the L word?"

I nod. "We have once, in the heat of the moment. I'm not sure if it's real. The physical side of things is strong. The friendly banter and long talks are amazing. But can that translate into a lifetime commitment when our backgrounds are so different? He's had tragedy in his life, and I've never even had a committed relationship. There's a lot to consider."

"And I always thought I'd envy someone who'd snagged a secret billionaire in a small-town bakery. Yet here I am feeling sorry for you."

We both laugh and I feel my worries subside a little. Being with Bailey always helps me stay positive.

"We should look at what they're saying. Online."

I let out a heavy breath. "Okay. Let's do this." My stomach churns again and I gulp my water. "You know what? I don't want to. Not yet."

I don't even want to ask Julian about it yet. At least I can get meeting his family out of the way first. But I do have some niggling doubts and I'd like to talk to him about those. For now, I'm blocking out the white noise. "I want to ask Julian about it first. Give him the benefit of the doubt."

"You look pale. Maybe you should lie down for a bit. It could be jetlag. My sofa pulls out."

I nod. I do feel exhausted. "The sofa is fine as it is. No need to pull it out."

Bailey collects me a pillow and blanket. "Stay as long as you like. We can have the tacos later."

I nod and give a close-lipped smile. "Thanks Bailey."

I know I said I'd call Julian when I was ready but maybe I'm just fine here for the week. Maybe it's just too soon to make this call. My phone buzzes in my pocket.

*Thinking of you *love-heart emoji**

My heart soars with emotion. I know I have strong feelings for him. Facing things head on is what I always do. I touch the emoji with love-heart eyes and send that back.

Who knew a relationship status could cause so many confused and amazing feelings at once?

17

Chapter Seventeen

JULIAN

Three days after I'd told the parents I was bringing Sofia home, we're on the expansive marble doorstep of Blackwood Estate.

"I'm not sure what I expected, but it certainly wasn't this. Your home is huge!"

"Tell me about it." He rolls his eyes. "But I can assure you a normal family lives in here. By the way, at some point, the parents will organize a family dinner. I'm sorry in advance and I will attempt to make it as low-key as possible."

"That's fine. I'd love to meet your whole family."

"Just be careful what you wish for."

I turn the door handle as Sofia touches me on the arm, her eyes glittering at me as she speaks. "Julian, there's stuff online about you and my green card. I haven't read it, so I'm not sure of the actual context. But I just need to know, you didn't manipulate that in any way, did you?"

"No, I mean..." Then the door is pulled open from the inside and as it swings open, I see my whole family, including nieces and nephews staring back at me.

"Surprise!" They all yell in unison.

"What the actual f—" Then I look at the kids. "farmyard... are you all doing? You know I hate surprises."

The kids pull party poppers and tiny streamers spread everywhere.

My three brothers Darien, Brock, and Mitchell give me the double thumbs up from behind everyone, stupidly proud grins plastered across their faces.

"You're welcome, brother." Darien says with a laugh. "We couldn't miss the eldest moving back home, could we?

"Meatheads," I growl. "It's temporary."

"Don't worry, kid-dults are a real thing. No need to be ashamed." I'm sure Mom still has your pacifier stashed somewhere," the second eldest, Mitchell, explains like I'm a child. His wife, Karina, hits him in the arm which just makes him laugh.

"He's not a kid-dult. I think he's more of a man-child." He leans over and pushes me on the shoulder. "Don't just stand there looking broody. Introduce us to this poor woman." Brock the second youngest says.

It's a damned conspiracy.

"Honestly, you men." Eva, Brock's wife, speaks up. "Come on, Sofia. We'll leave them to it." She reaches out for Sofia's hand and I can see the amusement in her eyes. "Kids, come with us. You can play with Uncle Julian outside later. Then Eva, Karina and Sofia walk off into the foyer and towards the family room followed by the six children. Two of them are Brock's and the other four are Mitchell's.

"Unbelievable." I step inside. "Mom, we agreed on low-key. Now Sofia gets accosted on the first day."

"Your brothers insisted you'd really appreciate it. I know deep down you do. I'm going to make salads. Charles, come and help please. Let the boys have a catch up."

"Of course."

"Not to worry, son. Sofia has to meet everyone eventually. Always better to rip that sticking plaster off quickly." Dad says as he follows Mom to the kitchen.

"Thanks for the advice." I don't try and hide my sarcasm.

"Come on, let's go get a beer," Darien suggests.

"It's midday, Darien. Okay for you; you don't have kids to worry about." Mitchell says.

"Exactly," Brock agrees, "and beer breath is a sexual buzzkill. So it's a no from me. Maybe you should try a soda."

"I feel attacked for my life choices. I need a beer now so I can handle the pressure," Darien says with feigned concern. "At least my biggest bro can drink with me."

I'm not falling for that again. Last time I ended up on the wrong side of a dozen empty beer bottles and howling at the moon with him. "No beers for me. I'll be helping Sofia get settled in after dinner."

"Hah!" Darien lightly pushes me from behind. "*Get settled in*. Nice one. I'm sure you'll settle her in *real* good."

My temper flares. I spin around to Darien behind me "Don't you ever speak about Sofia like that again."

His face deadpans. "You're right, bro. That was uncalled for. Sorry."

That's one thing about Darien. He always owns his shit. Commendable because he had a lot of shit to own. You have to admire a man who can live his life so unapologetically. But did the media beat him up about it? Of course not. They love his devil-may-care attitude and revel in all things Darien Blackwood. That used to annoy the crap out of me. I couldn't breathe without it being front-page news.

I nod my acceptance of his apology and go towards the family room to check in on Sofia. "I'll be out there shortly."

I need to get her aside and tell her about the green card. I wish I'd told her before. I should have. But really all I did was ask a question and suggest it could be posted sooner rather than later. I pause a minute and pull out my cell phone and bring up my socials.

How would something like that even get leaked? I'm sure my previous client who told me the green card had been approved a month ago is rock solid. Maybe it's just stuff that's been made up because they found out Sofia got a green card. I read some of the headlines.

Green card deal for Julian Blackwood

Overnight success model has connections of the Blackwood kind

Who is Sofia Fernandez and how badly did she want her green card?

My temper launches first and I shut my phone off and take a breath. I promised Sofia I wouldn't let this get to me. I have to stay calm. I stride into the family room and all the children are gathered around her. My heart almost stops as the thought of this being my future flashes through my head.

My own family. A wife. A home we can make together. As if she senses my gaze on her she lifts her eyes to mine and smiles. A thrill races though me. I'd give anything to have a family with her; for her to be my family. I don't even know if she wants kids, or marriage.

"Just checking in. Your bags have been taken to the guest wing. When you're ready, I'll take you there." She looks a little drawn around the eyes and I know she had a couple of nights on Bailey's sofa. Perhaps she needs some proper sleep.

"You know what? This has been an amazing greeting, but I think I'll go deal with my things and pop back shortly. Is that okay with you ladies?" Her smile beams and her dark hair shines against her red dress.

"We'll go and help with the food and meet you out on the back deck. Take whatever time you need." Karina says with a smile.

Sofia gets up and I take her hand. "See you all out back soon." I say feeling relieved I have the chance to speak with Sofia in private.

She's studying the artworks along the hallway. "Who's the art enthusiast, apart from you?"

"Both Mom and Dad."

"Yet you said they didn't want art for you?"

"As a hobby, yes. But as a career, no way. But we've moved past that, finally. You helped me see where I could do things differently. That helped."

"I'm glad. How far away is this guest room?"

"The guest wing is along this corridor and to the left." I use my arm to show the direction.

"I can't believe there are homes like this in real life."

We make it to the doorway into the guest quarters and I open it. "After you."

Sofia walks in and I hear her gasp.

"Will this be okay?"

"Of course. It's too much. Can't we just have a room."

I shake my head. "More privacy here." I know Mom wouldn't purposely listen in but if she happened to hear a conversation, or anything else, she may not stop listening," I grin at Sofia who isn't the quietest in the throes of passion, and apparently neither am I. "I want to talk about the green card thing."

Her gaze pins me. "You say that like I have something to be worried about."

"No, look. We agreed this stuff wouldn't derail us. I should have told you before, but I honestly didn't think it mattered. But now all this speculation has come out, and we've talked about how you feel about communication, I can see how me not mentioning it could be negative."

"Did you have anything to do with me getting my green card?"

"No. Not with the approval. But I have a connection in the embassy, and I asked him to see how yours was progressing."

Sofia's dark eyes are still drilling me.

"And... he did a search to find out it had been approved a month before that. I suggested getting it sent sooner rather than later would be a personal favor to me."

"So I did get it because of you?"

"No. You already had approval. No one can possibly chase that up and come up with anything to suggest I manipulated it in any way. I promise."

"I believe you. Thanks for telling me now. Have you read what's online?"

"I had a quick look. It all seems more like speculation because you're here from another country and you'd applied for a green card. Because I'm now linked to you, you've landed a major modeling gig, and I'm a billionaire back from being missing in action, they've put two and two together and come up with six."

"I guess this is my first taste of being scrutinized publicly."

"I wish I could save you from all of it."

"I just ask that you keep the honesty flowing. Any small thing can get blown out of proportion, so we need to tell each other anything. No decisions until we've talked to each other first."

"Agreed. Go take a quick look around and we'll head out back. These kids are dying to attack me, and I know Mom wants to get to know you." I give her a hug and genuine affection floods over me. I just want this to work so badly.

"Sounds fabulous. I hope they like me and can see I have genuine feelings for you."

I squeeze her a little bit tighter. "You do?"

She nods as she looks into my eyes. "Yes."

"Things may get tricky after our red-carpet premiere."

"Only way through it is to do it."

***

"Sofia, Julian said you met in a bakery? Did you do the baking?" Mom asks Sofia after dinner when we find ourselves alone at the table.

"I wasn't the actual baker. I did a little of everything. But I did love making new pastries and helping the baker out with everything. I learned a lot, and the customers really seemed to love my baking."

"I'm sure you'll put my cookies to shame." Mom says.

"I just had one and I can tell you, they are every bit as good as any bakery cookie I've ever had."

Mom smiles. "You're too kind, I'm sure. Where did you learn to bake?"

"My mother taught me. She's excellent with pastries and cakes."

"Forgive me if I'm being nosy, but does your mother still live in Argentina?"

I'm praying Mom doesn't open up her mouth and put her foot in it.

"Yes, with my father and four younger sisters."

"Why did you want to come to the USA?"

Sofia shrugs. "Usual reasons. The American dream in a way I suppose, and some family issues at the time."

"Mom, this can wait. We haven't even had dessert." I interrupt.

"It's fine, Julian. I got this." Sofia flashes a glare at me.

I sit back and take her word that she can handle this, but I'm damned nervous Mom will say something offensive without meaning to.

"I've nothing to hide, Mrs. Blackwood. My aunt and uncle came out many years ago chasing the same American dream. They started out small and built up their business to the bakery that's in Artsbridge today."

"I see." Mom smiles. "They sound like hard workers."

"They worked *so* hard and sponsored some other family members to come here on working visas. We lost my beautiful aunt three years ago, and I'd been looking for a change—a chance to make changes with the youth at home. So I came out to help Uncle Carlos keep the bakery on its feet and see what the world here had to offer.

"And now?"

"That is a very long story I can tell you another day. But I can say I paint portraits and hope to sell my art one day. Thanks to the Artsbridge Charity Auction, I've now secured a modeling gig."

"I'd love to hear that story one day. You have a lot to be proud of."

"I have a lot to be thankful for." Sofia reaches out and touches my arm. "It's been really wonderful meeting you all and chatting but I really need to get some sleep. Will you think it's rude of me if I head back to the guest quarters?"

"Not at all. Here I'll pack some salad and chicken to take for later." Mom gets up and grabs the chicken platter.

"I appreciate that." I'll help bring the salads to the kitchen."

"Thank you, Sofia. I know we live in this palace, but I've always liked to keep up with everything myself. No staff." Mom gives Sofia a sideways smile. "I do have a big dishwashing machine..." she whispers loudly.

Sofia laughs. "I think you can allow that with all these hungry boys to feed, Mrs. Blackwood."

"Please, call me Lorraine."

I can really tell Mom likes Sofia and she fits in so easily with my brother and his wives. Dad hasn't said much but he hasn't warned me off her either, so that is a huge nod. I can't wait to snuggle up to her in bed tonight and just sleep. Waking up with her tomorrow morning will be the best. I'd like that on repeat times infinity.

18

Chapter Eighteen

SOFIA

I step onto the red carpet in Los Angeles in a golden dress and stilettos. Julian is beside me in a mad tuxedo that takes him to next level of hotness. He was right, I'm dripping in diamond, gold, and platinum jewelry and I'm feeling completely out of place despite my smiling and waving to the crowd and the cameras.

Julian stops for a minute. "Are you ready?"

"For what?"

"When we walk up there." He nods further along the carpets where the majority of media people are. "It will be a frenzy and the barrage of questions can take you by surprise. Do you want to check your messages before we go in?"

"Okay." I'm a little nervous. I look behind us and see Miriam who I'd met in D.C. that time. She's in a red pantsuit and looking amazing. She's alone. I smile at her and she nods back. No smile.

I look beyond her and there's no one else. "I thought you said you'd organize security?"

"I have. Miriam is right behind us."

"Miriam is the best security you have?" I'm not sure if he's joking or not.

"Miriam is the best everything I have." Then he squeezes my hand. "Except for you."

I want to kiss him but I stop myself. The days we'd shared in the guest quarters were amazing. He'd never once put pressure on me for more than cuddles and kisses. He wanted me to rest up. I must say, I do feel better for it. But my desire level is off the charts after a few days of being strung out like that. I pull out my cell phone and take a quick look. A message from my father. I'm not sure whether to read it or not.

But I click into it and see

Congrats, Sofia. I'm so proud of you tonight!

Wow, okay. Dad is finally acknowledging an achievement of mine. I text him back.

Thanks, Dad

My phone buzzes again, shortly after. I take a look.

Julian Blackwood. I knew you could do it

Wait. He's congratulating me on being with Julian, not for this modeling job or anything I've done to get this far; just that I have a billionaire on my arm. My heart sinks. I'd actually believed for a second, I'd made him proud of me, the woman. I stuff my phone back into my purse. "Let's get this walk over with."

"Remember to say nice things about the company you're here for."

I hold Julian's arm as we progress into the thick of the media as we move along the red carpet.

The flashes are blinding and our names are called out constantly. I have my cues of where to stop and answer questions to satisfy the company and I'm mostly nodding and smiling and trying to own this whole red carpet rush.

I use some personal flair for any questions directed at me, but always finish with a practiced response. Finally, we are inside the Sofitel Hotel in Beverly Hills. I suck in a breath and gaze around. Everything about the place exudes rich, extravagant luxury.

We're seated up front at a dinner table with some very important people, so I've been told. I don't know any of them. But any one of them may be a step up into the art world for me.

"Roger." Julian nods to one man as I sit down.

He does a double take. "Well, well. *The* Julian Blackwood. What a pleasant surprise."

I get the feeling it's no surprise at all, but I've no idea why.

"I wish I could say the same." Julian says curtly. "This is Roger Birch. Reporter."

"Oh, come now, far from a reporter. I head up my own media company these days. You haven't been hiding away that long, Julian. I see you."

"I'm happy for you," Julian answers in a bland tone.

Clearly no love lost between these two.

I'm whisked off to meet some more people in the industry. I'm not really sure what's going on with Julian and whoever Roger is, but I can sense Julian is not happy. I excuse myself and head back towards my seat. I am stopped by another person, a woman who introduces herself as a fashion magazine editor. I can hear Roger as I'm chatting. I'm close enough to hear Roger and I can see them both.

"Oh now, let's let bygones be bygones. I see you're back as good as new. And with a stunning new lady. I mean the chances of history repeating itself is slim to none, surely?" Roger's smarmy voice says.

"Why are you torturing me? Just go away. You being at Sofia's table is no coincidence, I bet."

"Because a scoop is a scoop and that's what I live for. So you're done being Jack?"

"No comment."

"Is it serious between you and Miss Fernandez? I mean, you have a lot to offer her. A lot of strings you can pull. Private lessons? Maybe an engagement ring soon." He winks at Julian.

"We're friends. That's all. Now go crawl back under a rock. Excuse me." Julian gets up and walks off.

Friends? So much for us having each other's back. Julian has bailed out on me the second things get tough. Why did I believe he would stand up for us when he said he would? The very first confrontation with media and he can't admit he has feelings for me. Disappointment hits me. I excuse myself from the rambling lady and sit at the table with Roger.

"This is your big night, Sofia. You should be very proud for some-one with your background."

I level him with my gaze but say nothing.

"What do you mean by that, Birch?" Julian snaps as he comes back to be seated.

"Nothing at all. Not every day an Artsbridge baker's assistant from Argentina manages to get the brooding artist out of his cave."

Julian clenches his fists. I can't help but wonder how Roger knows those details? What exactly did Julian say to him while I couldn't hear?

"I mean the model auction for the charity gala was a lucky break. Being bought for all that money," Roger addresses me now.

"If you are referring to the fact that Julian bought me, yes, I already know. Move along." I say.

"His first wife was a nude model for him as well. Funny how history repeats. But you probably knew that too."

I look at Roger and then at Julian. Then back at Roger. "I'm sure we aren't here to hear about Julian's past. You should find some new material, Mr. Birch."

"I know but there's just so much good stuff in the past."

"Shut up, Birch. Or I'll shut you up." Julian says through gritted teeth.

Other guests at our table are chatting and laughing and suddenly seem to get what's going on here. Miriam is behind Julian now.

Roger laughs again. "Temper, temper, Julian. You don't want your new girlfriend seeing the real you. Did you buy Sofia's naked portrait just like Tilly's, to add to your private collection? Of course, you know about his extensive private collection of exes he's painted nude."

"She isn't my girlfriend. We're friends. That's all." Julian states. "Stop spewing your poison."

"I think you should find another table to sit at." I tell Roger. Then I look at Julian, "Or maybe *we* should."

"This is your night, and this is your table. He can fucking leave," Julian seethes and Miriam closes in to the table.

Roger looks up at Miriam who is bringing a new meaning to death stares as he speaks to her.

"Ah, I see you still have your watchdog. Miriam, aren't you getting a little old for this game?"

"Perhaps you'd like me to prove I'm not," Miriam answers. "Julian, do you have a minute? There's someone who wants to catch up."

"Yes, you best let yourself get rounded up before you do something that you'll regret and I'll love spreading to the world."

"I can absolutely assure you I won't regret it one bit." Julian walks over and grabs Roger by the shirtfront. Miriam intervenes and Julian lets go.

Roger stands up and raises his hands. "Fine, fine. I'm going. I'll be seeing you around."

"Not if I see you first." Julian says.

"That's just it. You don't see me first. You never see me coming literally or figuratively."

"Piss off."

"Enjoy your night." He tips his hat to me and walks off. "Enjoy being owned by Julian Blackwood. Perhaps you should ask to see his private collection."

"Whatever I ask of Julian has nothing to do with you. The past is in the past. It's a little sad that you see a need to live in it, Mr. Birch. Perhaps you should spend more time training how to be a real journalist who can affect change in the world instead of a deadbeat reporter making up stories that hurt people." I state as he walks off.

He turns back to me. "There's always some truth in what I report." He smiles a discomforting smile. "But you're new to all of this, aren't you? The best advice I can give is, where there's smoke there's fire, so don't trust anyone making money off you. All publicity is good publicity. I didn't get this seat by accident, Miss Fernandez."

He leaves and the people at the table go back to chatting and then they get up to mingle and no doubt gossip about what they've just witnessed.

"Julian, are you okay." I've seen him angry but not like this.

"I hate that ass. He's been a thorn for years."

"Maybe you should leave, Julian," Miriam suggests.

"No! I'm not running away from this shit anymore," Julian snaps and Miriam backs away from him.

"Why does he have it in for you?" I ask.

Julian sighs. "I dated his sister once. She's lovely, but also has that dogged determination to make something the truth even if it isn't."

"Must run in the family."

"Anyway, she wanted me to paint her. I called it off and apparently broke her heart. He's had it in for me ever since. This was back in my early days as a portrait artist. I had talent but I was Julian Blackwood heir to billions blah, blah. There was no shortage of young women wanting to be painted but none of them cared about my talent. I enjoyed the attention for a while and chose my favorites to paint as nudes. But that lifestyle went when I met and married Tilly. Instead of leaving us to live our lives, he was relentless in reporting on Tilly."

"I see. Why did you say we're just friends?"

"To protect you. You don't know what he's capable of."

"I thought we'd agreed. We have nothing to hide." I can't shake the feeling I don't belong here with Julian, but I'm not walking out on this launch. "Let them say what they want to say. But now I think you do have a lot you're still hiding. A lot of unresolved feelings. You're not ready to move your life forward."

"That's not true." He leans in closer, his voice low. I want to move forward with you."

"Except you just let him get to you and you went against what we'd agreed. I'm not even sure we can be friends at this point, Julian. I can get myself to my room and also back to Argentina. I feel the tears stinging at my eyes. I love this man but I need to be true to myself. He needs to finish his journey and be true to himself. This just isn't the right timing for us. I'm not sure it will ever be.

"Don't do this, Sofia. You know I love you."

"You did this and sometimes... *this* time, love just isn't enough."

"I don't believe that. I think this is exactly our time and I'm going to prove it to you."

"I just need some space right now. I need to be on stage soon. I think you should leave."

19

Chapter Nineteen

JULIAN

Two months later

"Are you still moping?" Miriam asks when I walk into her office in D.C.

"Far from it. I had a haircut and a shave, so don't worry, Miriam. I'm not going back to being a recluse," I grin. "Actually, these past few months have been the best."

"What about Sofia?"

"I'm going to see her next week. I'm not taking no for an answer. I've written everything there is to know about me, every part of me, down and I've given it to her. There's nothing she won't know about my past."

"That must be one hell of a document. Probably fill a semi-trailer. It is the way to go. Being open and honest with her. She's very proud. Has a lot of integrity. You can't whitewash her. If you're not being one hundred percent honest, she'll know. But more to the point, you'll know." Miriam as always gives her no-nonsense, sage advice.

"I get that. She was right. I still had a lot to unpack. I've done that now. Writing it all down, understanding who I am, understanding who I want to be, has been just what I needed. Some of it is a work in progress."

"Has Sofia read all of this epiphany?"

"I've sent her the file. I'm not sure how much she's read. I don't care. We've been communicating every day. The first week she was distant but I told her I want her in my life, even as just a friend and that I wouldn't try and cross any line for the sake of my ego. I miss being around her."

"That's a huge leap for you."

I nod, but it seems like it should never have been anything huge. I've tried to let her have personal space and just been supportive as a friend. Like we used to be in Artsbridge. I've missed that."

"How are the cottages coming along?"

"They aren't done yet, but I'm happy with how they are shaping up. Living back home has actually been fine. I've gone through my old room and gotten rid of that stupid private collection. Amazing how a good bonfire can cleanse the soul. I only have Sofia's portrait now, in storage. She has an official opening of her first youth support and learning center tomorrow night and I intend to be there. The bakery is shutting down for the weekend and I'm flying everyone there. Her best friends want to support her."

"Good luck, Julian. I hope you find your happiness."

"There's just no one else for me. If we are only ever friends, I'll accept that. But not before I try everything to win her heart back."

***

Buenos Aires
  Two days later

I'm standing outside Sofia's family home. My heart is racing as I knock. Will she answer the door? Seeing her after all this time still excites me more than anything in the world. Her mother opens the door.

"Julian. I wasn't expecting you. I guess Sofia doesn't know you're here."

I shake my head. "Sorry, but I wanted it to be a surprise, for her opening tomorrow. I've flown all her friends down here from the bakery. They want to support her."

"That's a beautiful gesture. I'm sure she will appreciate it. She's missed them. And you, I suspect. More than she's letting on. Come in."

"Is she home?" I step inside the door and we go to the kitchen and sit.

"No. After her modeling finished with Rialto, she bought a small apartment of her own. Somewhere she can do her portrait work."

"She hadn't mentioned she'd moved."

"She only went yesterday and she's been a little preoccupied since she got back. She and her father find it a little hard to co-exist. I wish that man was a little less traditional sometimes. But it is what it is."

"They are very different, aren't they?"

She nods. "They have the same determination; it's just their views clash. She's trying hard to make him proud of her as a successful woman. He wants to see her secure and happy with a man who can give her everything that we never had as children or a young couple."

"I see both points, but this is part of who Sofia is. Maybe it's her belief in herself we need to work on. Does *she* feel she's enough to warrant having amazing things?"

"I guess that's where you come in, Julian. Don't give up on her. Just understand her and let her be who she was born to be. Don't judge her, but accept her. All of her."

I nod. This is what I've always craved. I know exactly how she feels. Time to go and show her she will always be enough for me, no matter what she chooses to do.

"Don't tell her I'm here. Everyone else will sleep now and surprise her at the opening tomorrow. I wonder if you would give me her address. I have a surprise of my own."

Sofia's mother smiles. "I'll write it down. She'll be at home resting for tomorrow. It's been a hectic month."

"She might kick me out yet, but I have to try."

"Good luck."

***

Sofia opens the door in the not-so-amazing apartment block when I knock. The first thing I see are those amazing eyes and her skin is actually glowing.

"Julian! What the heck?"

"Surprise! I wanted to be here for tomorrow." I let my gaze run down her body. Except her usual body hugging attire has been replaced by a loose dress and my gaze lingers on her abdomen. There's more swell than usual.

Her hands are now cupping under her belly. "I guess I'm not the only one getting a surprise."

My brain can hardly comprehend what this means but I also know exactly what this means. I drop to my knees on the floor in front of her. Leaning my head against the soft bump. "Sofia, this is my baby? You're having my baby?" Tears prickle my eyes. All the pain of the unknown baby I'd lost washes over me. I'm getting a second chance and I'm not stuffing this up. I'll become a pauper if it means I get my family with Sofia.

She laughs softly. "Yes. I wasn't sure what you'd think. I have my plane ticket booked to come and see you. I just needed to be here for tomorrow."

I stand up and draw her into my arms. "You win the surprises today. I wish you'd told me, but I get why you didn't. You didn't need two babies to raise. But I'm good, Sofia. I really am. Did you read all about me and my past?" I ask and she nods, so I kiss her forehead and keep talking. "I know I want you in my life forever and if that means just as co-parents or as friends, I'll take it. You are the only woman for me."

"I'm sorry I reacted the way I did. I guess I had some things to work out for myself, too. When my father sent me a text congratulating me on landing you, it threw me off-kilter. I was confused about what I wanted."

"He did what? Why didn't you tell me?" We walk into her small space.

"I'm not sure. I just didn't want to admit his opinion still affected me so much. I could advise you on how to deal with personal issues but I couldn't take that advice for myself. Now I see, what's really important is how I feel about myself."

"How do you feel about you?"

"Like I deserve everything in the world and this baby needs two happy parents to raise him."

"Him? We're having a boy?" Everything in me almost bursts. "A happy, healthy child is all I want. Boy or girl doesn't matter, but it's so cool to know. Please, Sofia. Be with me as more than friends."

"Friends with benefits?"

We both laugh. "I want you to marry me. But you do you. However you want this to happen, we can make it happen. I love you more than this whole world. I love our baby and I want us to be a family. We can live wherever you choose and you can be a model, or an artist, or a pastry chef. Be a cleaner. Hell, I don't care. Just be mine."

"I love you too, Julian. You are a good man. You help me be a better person. I'd love us to be a family together however, that works out."

I pull her close to me where she belongs and where she is going to stay. The mother of my first-born child. The other half of me. This is truly living.

EPILOGUE

SOFIA

"Watercolors are hard." I say to Julian who's standing at his own easel next to me. We're at the beach on a massive family vacation. Okay it's the private beach at our vacation home but with our size of extended family, there's not room on a public beach.

"I know, right? The colors just have a mind of their own. But I'm glad you suggested we try something new." Julian smiles at me.

"I can assure you young Jack isn't getting near oil colors. I don't need permanent abstracts on the walls." I laugh and we both look down at our two-year-old, slapping paint on his own small easel between us.

"I think he has my talent for abstracts," Julian observes.

"I think he'll have your talent for everything. You're amazing at teaching him. You're so patient."

"You are the amazing one. Look at how clever you are," he says as he rubs his hand over my very swollen bump. "Growing us a little sister. I hope she has your hair and eyes."

I cradle the bump and she kicks at my hand. "She sure likes her own space, so I think she'll take after you." I grin at my gorgeous husband.

"Sis, sis," Jack says as he touches my belly.

"Yes, Jack. Your baby sister will be out to meet you soon."

He grins and drops his paintbrush, making a beeline for the waves.

"Julian, catch him quick!" I cry out, knowing I have no hope to get to his superfast toddler legs before he reaches the surf. It's not dangerous, but it can still put him off balance.

Julian has already launched into action and he scoops up our son and places him on his shoulders. "Come on! Daddy will take you for a swim."

"Yay! Swim." Jack giggles as they run down the beach and join in with our nephews and nieces. I look up the beach and wave to my three younger sisters, the youngest having just reached official teenager age. They all wave back. It's amazing to have them all here with me for a vacation. It's the first time since our wedding that my family and Julian's family are together.

"How are you feeling, Sofia?" Lorraine asks as she hands me a glass of iced water. "I think you should rest in the shade for a while. You've been standing in the sun for hours."

"I do have a hat and sunscreen on. But, you're probably right. I might come and rest up. My feet are swelling a little. Where are the others?"

"Your parents have just popped out to the shops for some ice cream and Charles is reading a book." She points to Julian's dad with a book over his face in the deck lounger. "Also known as sleeping."

We laugh. My other boys are off sneaking a beer they think we women know nothing about, and I think your friends Bailey and Rob have just arrived and gone to get changed into their swimsuits."

I smile. "Oh, have they?" Bailey loathes the sand and the beach, but I think it's one of the few places where she and Rob can relax and be themselves. I can't help but wish the same happiness for Bailey and Rob. Those two have taken two steps forward and one step backward.

Finally, those two have actually set a wedding date and Bailey is in the midst of planning what I jokingly call, "The Wedding of the Century."

I sit in a chair under the umbrella and sip my water while I watch Rob sets up a huge umbrella and beach chairs while Bailey approaches. I chuckle at the way she ignores Julian's youngest brother, Darien. Ever since being introduced to each other, Bailey and Darien seem to rub each other the wrong way.

"Hey, Sofia," she greets me. "Thanks for the invite. Sorry we're late to the party. I had some business to take care of online. You and Julian now have one hundred thousand followers and there's some baby stuff arriving from companies next week for you to use and review."

"You can stop working, you know." I say to her. "That's some bikini you have on."

She shrugs. Nothing special. It's the beach. I thought I'd play my part."

"Good for you."

Just like a moth to a flame I see Darien coming towards us. "They'll let anyone on this beach, won't they?"

Bailey spins around to face him. "Well, you're here, so they can't be fussy." Then she struts off with all her ample assets moving in a particular way that appeals to men. It certainly seems to appeal to Darien as I observe his gaze following her until she's out of sight behind her giant beach umbrella.

I grin and shake my head. Julian swears that Darien is the perpetual bachelor, but it's so obvious that he finds the still very much engaged Bailey, fascinating.

Then I feel drops of cold water. "Hey!" I start as Julian sits beside me.

"Sorry. Jack is making a sandcastle with the kids. They are just down there, see?" He points at the group.

I nod. The older teens are there too, so he's safe.

"You doing okay, Mrs. Blackwood?" His hand closes over mine.

"I sure am, Mr. Blackwood."

"You know, you've made me the happiest man alive. You may not have saved my life when you stabbed me with that epiPen, but you certainly exchanged the miserable life I had for one far better than I had the courage to hope for."

"So you tell me every day." The words are light-hearted, but I feel such profound happiness and gratitude for how much I love this man and how much he loves me.

"I'll never stop telling you." He leans in and kisses me, pouring all the love he has for me into it.

I can never resist him and the craziness of hormones has the kiss deepening in no time.

Then I feel something down low, deep inside that isn't anything to do with my sexy husband.

I pull back. "Shit!"

"Oh, sorry. That bad was it?" He's joking around as I'm silently breathing through a contraction. Maybe it's Braxton Hicks? "Or is the young lass kicking up a storm as usual?"

The sensation dies off and I breathe. "Um, no it's all good. Just thought for a second I was—" Another searing cramping pain cuts off my words and takes my breath away. "Oh boy, oh boy. Oh shit." I say as I clutch at my belly.

"Sofia, are you okay? It can't be the baby, it's too soon."

I shake my head and then nod, still not able to focus on saying anything that makes sense.

"It is the baby?"

I nod as the pain subsides. "It's the baby. We should go to the hospital and check anyway."

Julian jumps up and runs towards the car park. "Shit!" He runs back and picks me up. "I better take you."

"Calm down. I'm fine."

"Mom, Dad! The baby!" Julian calls across the beach.

I think every person in the family moves towards us at once. My sister, Carmen is carrying Jack.

Julian takes me to our car. "Does everyone remember the drill?" he calls out as he puts me in the seat.

"Julian, no one has a drill to remember except for you. Jack will be fine. Just give him a hug and tell him he will see us soon. This could be nothing and I'll come back home tonight." I give Julian's hand a squeeze of encouragement.

Julian takes a deep breath and exhales slowly. "True. I'll go tell him."

Before I can shut the car door, Mom suddenly appears next to me. "Let me know if you need me there."

She's smiling but I also read a mother's anxiety in her eyes. I smile back. "I will Mom."

Julian comes back. "What if it is the baby coming? It's too soon, isn't it?"

"I'm just three weeks away from my due date, so she is perfectly safe to be born, even if it is a bit early." I reassure him. "It's better for me if you're calm. We've done this before, right?" This reassuring thing is tiring me out. I just want to get to the hospital and home again knowing our daughter is just fine, and if I come home with a little princess in my arms, then that's even better.

He looks at me. "Of course. We have, and look how amazing Jack is. Shall we go and see if we are going to meet our baby girl today?"

"Let's do that. I love you so much, Julian."

"I love you more, Sofia. More than I could imagine, more than the rest of my life."

The END

***

Dear Reader,

May I ask for a HUGE favor, please? If you enjoyed reading this book, would you please let me know by leaving a rating or even a review on Amazon? You can do so right here: https://www.amazon.com/review/create-review/?ie=UTF8 &channel=glance-detail&asin=B0D5PM5N6W   THANK YOU!

Hey, if you enjoyed reading, *Surprise Baby For the Secret Next Door Billionaire, guess what?* You'll LOVE my new steamy, hot mafia romance, *Silver Fox Billionaire Mob Boss*. Get your copy here: https://geni.us/MKFR91S

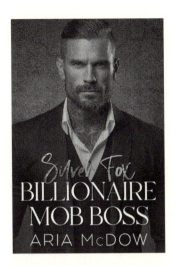

I fled into the arms of a mob boss for protection... and ended up pregnant by my father's sworn enemy.

I went to the club alone to dance away my stress when the ultimate stress reliever walked in.

At 6'4", he's rich, powerful, handsome, and old enough to be my dad.

His commanding presence and intense eyes drew me to him like a magnet.

Our mutual attraction led to one lust-filled night of heart-pounding, body-pumping passion.

The next day I was falsely accused of stealing from a violent drug cartel which put my life expectancy at zero.

Desperate, I'm forced to seek protection from a stranger.

Surprise! He's my one-night stand, mob boss Marco Tomacelli.

He became my savior as well as my new boss.

I swore to keep things professional, but he claimed me body and soul.

Dangerous enemies are coming for us both so his plan to leave the crime world behind is in jeopardy.

He has my heart and he has no clue he's knocked up the daughter of his ex-best friend and sworn enemy.

***

To stay in the know and be the first one to learn about my new releases, make sure to click the "Follow" button on the top left of my author's Amazon Page here: https://www.amazon.com/stores/Aria -McDow/author/B0C95F1Z59

The journey indeed goes on and on. Let's keep traveling the Yellow Book Road together!

Your Sneak Peak Is Next

Silver Fox Bilionaire Mob Boss

MARCO

The French Quarter of New Orleans, Louisiana, has an old and established reputation as the place to let loose. But anybody who is anybody knows that the French Quarter is strictly for tourists. If you're from New Orleans, you know the Uptown District rivals even Las Vegas.

Say what you want about Vegas, but if you are looking for Party Central, the Uptown District is the place to be.

Club 7114 is like any of the dozens of swanky nightclubs scattered across the Uptown District. Head-pounding, insistent techno beats pulsing out onto oak-lined streets, and the inside smelling like champagne, expensive cologne... and sex.

This is not my scene. It hasn't been for a long time. Hitting the clubs is more of a young man's game. In my line of work, however, you must go where your customers are.

The Marcellos, one of the last remaining families of the old guard, La Cosa Nostra, the Sicilian Mafia, once had a stranglehold on this city. Gambling, drugs, prostitution, strong-arming local businesses — we had it all covered once — but that's an ever-shrinking part of our business.

But old habits die hard.

The old phrase, 'crime doesn't pay,' has never been more accurate, especially when it comes to the problems that come with modern, high-tech policing and the incursion of the hyper-violent Mexican cartels.

The fact is, it used to be more profitable.

That doesn't necessarily mean I'm going legit; it's just that I target different markets with higher margins now.

Still, I keep up with what needs minding, and what needs minding right now is Club 7114.

I nod as I walk past the long line of hopefuls wanting to get in, right up to the door. As the underboss for the Marcellos New Orleans branch, I do not need to stand in line behind a velvet rope.

Simon, the bouncer, knows me by sight. He nods his head and greets me respectfully. "Good evening, Mr. Tomacelli."

"Evening, Simon," I say, stopping to ask, "How's little Joel doing?"

Joel is Simon's eight-year-old son who apparently fell off his skateboard and broke his leg in two places three weeks ago.

"He's a tough kid. He'll be fine," Simon answers without missing a beat, even though he knows he never told me what had happened to his kid.

No matter. I make it my business to know who, what, where, and how about my associates and their employees, as cultivating various relationships pays dividends.

"Good." I nod slightly and proceed to enter the club, the cacophony of music assaulting my senses. It's times like this I long for the old days when I used to consider this entertaining.

I see the person I came to speak with. Ricardo Santiago, longtime owner of Club 7114 sees me and is headed towards me.

"Little Marco," the old man is fond of calling me. He has known me from the time I was in high school. He pats me affectionately on the back. "Good to see you. Come to my office where it's quiet and we can have a drink."

I wave him off. "Another time, Old Man." I only want to deliver what was agreed upon, walk around the club, and go home. I withdraw an envelope from an inner pocket of my jacket and hand it to Ricardo who smoothly tucks it away.

"Thank you, Marco," he says, and there's no mistaking the sincere gratitude.

"Thank the Marcello family."

"I do," he says solemnly. "And I know which 'Marcello' to thank."

We shake hands and then go our separate ways. I head towards the dance floor, and he heads in the direction of his office.

The dance floor is the heart of the club. The space is dim, and colorful strobe lights glide over writhing bodies on the floor. Male and female, female and female, and male and male couples all dance with jerky, purposeless movements.

My gaze continues to roam until, suddenly, a solitary figure strikes me.

A beautiful young woman, dancing alone, lost in her world.

Unlike many other dancers, her moves are smooth, silky, almost serpentine.

Mesmerized, I stop and watch her.

She's wearing a short, shimmering red dress that hugs her shapely, perfectly proportioned curves like a second skin.

Her dress is tasteful, but one well-toned, bare shoulder intrigues me more than anything the other women on the dance floor have to offer. Their short, cut-out dresses leave nothing to the imagination.

Her mass of long, dark curls, flawless fair skin, and high, delicate cheekbones lend her an air of classic beauty, so much different from any of the other young women.

She's lost in her dance. Her eyes are closed, and I long to know their color and depth.

Immediately, I know I want to have her.

I make up my mind that I will win her because I know that I can.

I don't deny that women find me attractive. I work hard for that. At age 42, I'm in peak physical condition. I don't have to work hard to draw women to me, even if some of that is because I'm worth more than the economy of some small countries.

Eventually, I tear my gaze away and press through the crowd toward the raised platform at the back of the room and the VIP seating.

Frowning, I see three Jalisco Mexican cartel men seated at the table reserved at all times for members of the Marcello family.

Each man at my table has a beautiful, attentive woman sitting on his lap.

Glasses of all varieties of cocktails clutter the table, as does one unopened bottle of 1998 Dom Perignon Rose.

Of all the Mexican cartels that have become part of the trafficking scene in New Orleans in the last couple of years, the Jalisco cartel is the worst of the worst.

But the Marcellos have a habit of steering clear.

Jalisco cockroaches trying to move into the upscale club scene are beneath me. They are uneducated and untrained, and while extremely violent, they just weren't worth the effort to squash when, on their own, they command enough attention from the police.

Right now, though, I want my table, and what I want, I take.

"Gentlemen, you're at my table. I require it now. There's an empty table," I gesture to a non-VIP table across the room. "It's over there."

Predictably, two men unceremoniously shove away the women attending them and stand up menacingly, while the third merely looks at me with recognition in his eyes.

The two standing men look me over and begin a dialogue amongst themselves. "José," one says to the other, "this man is talking crazy, but do you think he knows he's crazy?"

"He doesn't look crazy, yet he must be. Otherwise, he would not act like he wanted to have his face peeled off tonight," José answers.

I know that in exactly 30 seconds, guns, knives, or fists are coming out — and while I'm outnumbered and these men are younger — I have no fear. I can handle this situation, and my face will remain intact.

At this moment, the third member of the Jalisco cartel, still seated, reaches out his hand and grabs hold of the man's arm to his right. "Be still," he commands quietly as if accurately reading the 'I-don't-give-a-fuck-if-I-have-to-kill-you-now' message in my eyes.

"Do you know who this is?" the apparent leader asks his companions.

For a moment, the two men look at each other in confusion. Danger is still in the air, but now there is uncertainty. "This is Gianmarco Tomacelli, underboss of the Marcello crime family's New Orleans branch," the seated man informs.

Without waiting for a response, the Jalisco leader continues. "We are going. For now. But don't worry; there will be a time when the Jalisco Cartel will wipe away Marcello's influence until they come crawling to us like dogs for our leftover crumbs." He gets to his feet and makes to leave.

"Have a pleasant evening," I say, but I don't move, forcing the men and their pouting women to walk around me.

The danger has passed.

I know that my associates who work in the club could have come to my defense, but still, I can feel the adrenaline leaving my body.

I'm getting too old for this shit.

I sit down and open the bottle of expensive champagne they fortuitously left behind. I signal the nearest waitstaff to come bus the table, and bring me some clean glasses. In short order, it is as if the table had not been occupied a mere five minutes ago. That's when I notice the table across from me is no longer empty. The beautiful woman I had seen on the dance floor is sitting there and alone.

I pick up two glasses and the bottle and walk over to her table.

Up here, the music is still loud, but the noise level is less overwhelming, making some conversation possible. I lean over close so that she can hear me. "Hello," I say, laying on my smoothest tone. "I couldn't help but notice you out here alone."

She doesn't seem all that impressed, looking me over with an air of indifference, if not outright disdain.

That was unusual but also incredibly sexy. Sometimes, it was the women who made me make an effort to get to know them who appealed to me most.

"*Por qué me molestas?*" Seeing my confusion, she pauses and translates into English, "Why are you bothering me?"

Then, there it is. That telltale glint in her eye that lets me know she's interested.

She's good, but I have the edge on her in the experience department.

Speaking of experience, *She's young enough to be your daughter.* My conscience picks this moment to weigh in, but I'm too intrigued by her beauty to listen.

"Looks to me like you're not too bothered by me," I say, not taking my eyes from hers.

"Maybe." A hint of a smile is playing at the corners of her mouth.

Yeah, she's interested.

"I thought maybe you'd like to go someplace a little quieter," I say.

"Why is that?" she asks, raising an eyebrow.

Such beautiful, liquid-brown eyes.

"Because apparently, all of the men in here are blind fools. A beautiful woman like you deserves someone who knows how to show her some appreciation. I know the perfect place," I say, my thoughts turning to the promise the rest of the evening offered.

She appears to turn that over in her mind for a moment before responding, and I wait patiently for her to complete her analysis.

When she does, one corner of her mouth quirks up before her full, gorgeous lips part to speak. "How do I know you're not some serial killer?"

I laugh loudly and deeply and say, "You don't."

Two minutes later, as we leave, I notice her glance towards the same Jalisco Cartel men I ousted from my table and who are now congregating in the back. Could mean something. Could mean nothing. I keep it moving and file it away for future consideration.

***

I had entered the club solo; now I am leaving with a beautiful young woman on my arm.

She's had more than a drink or two, but she isn't drunk.

This is a scene Vittorio, my driver, has seen many times before. He greets us at my car, waiting by the opened back door.

Vittorio, a man old enough to remember both the good old days and the bad, is the soul of discretion. His eyes and ears see all, but what he knows, he keeps well to himself... unless I ask him.

Something about how he looks from the woman to me tells me that this is the time for me to ask what's on his mind.

I consider the possibilities while she slides across the back seat, exchanging small talk.

She laughs, and her breath smells of Sangria, not the bottle of champagne, abandoned for a second time.

I don't know this woman, not even her name.

I have heard from a reputable source that Alberto Valero, the head of the Jalisco cartel, has a new mule, a beautiful young woman, working for him.

The way she looked at the Jalisco men as we were leaving... maybe it's her. Who knows? I've never met her, or Valero, for that matter.

If she is the same person, messing with someone who works for his organization could be very bad for my health.

Valero is known to be the jealous type and doesn't like outsiders.

But now, with this beauty on my arm, her smell is so intoxicating, I don't care. Fuck Valero, I can handle him.

Before I slide into my car, Vittorio leans in and says, in a low voice, "Be careful, Mr. Tomacelli."

***

The trip to my home was exciting and seemed excruciatingly long.

Her tongue was down my throat.

My hands were under her dress.

We came up for air and my hands stopped teasing her perfectly pert breasts while Vittorio took the limo a little harder around a corner than was strictly necessary, causing our bodies to smash up against the door.

I signaled my displeasure by rapping the ceiling sharply.

Vittorio's gaze met mine in the rearview mirror. "Sorry, Boss," he said, not entirely hiding the smirk in his eyes.

Vittorio was not entirely wrong. I'd been exchanging saliva for over 20 minutes with a nameless stranger inside a dark car. What a poor display of gentlemanly manners. "What is your name?"

"Call me Nik," she said.

"Is that your real name?" I asked, curious. "How do I know if it is?"

She laughed and threw my earlier words back in my face. "You don't."

A few minutes later, Vittorio steered the car through the security gates of my sprawling compound. When the vehicle stopped in the circular driveway before the main doors, Nik's head rested on my shoulder, and my fingers stroked through the delicate ringlets of her flowing, dark mane.

"We're here. Ready to take the party upstairs?"

Her answer was another scorching kiss, her tongue gliding across my teeth, tickling my palate.

I growled low in my throat and grabbed her head, my cock straining in my linen pants.

She wanted it, and I'm going to give it to her.

When we emerged, Vittorio opened the car door but didn't say a word.

I have long silenced the niggling urge in the back of my brain to ask Vittorio if he has something he wants to tell me.

***

Ready to read for FREE? Get your FREE copy right here: https://dl.bookfunnel.com/42v0kof218

Made in the USA
Columbia, SC
28 September 2024

43126534R00114